Sabine Baring-Gould

**Richard Cable**

Vol. 3

Sabine Baring-Gould

**Richard Cable**
*Vol. 3*

ISBN/EAN: 9783337253639

Printed in Europe, USA, Canada, Australia, Japan

Cover: Foto ©Raphael Reischuk / pixelio.de

More available books at **www.hansebooks.com**

# RICHARD CABLE

VOL. III.

# RICHARD CABLE

## THE LIGHTSHIPMAN

BY THE AUTHOR OF

'MEHALAH' 'JOHN HERRING' 'COURT ROYAL'
ETC.

IN THREE VOLUMES

VOL. III.

LONDON
SMITH, ELDER, & CO., 15 WATERLOO PLACE
1888

# CONTENTS

OF

## THE THIRD VOLUME.

# RICHARD CABLE.

## CHAPTER XLII.

### A GOLDEN PLUM.

NOTHING is more simple. Fortune sits on a cloud and lets down golden plums suspended by a hair into this nether world of ours. Those of us who are wide-awake and on the look-out for plums, the moment we see the golden drop descend, dash past our neighbours, kick their shins to make them step aside, tread them down if they obstruct our course, jostle them apart, and before they have pulled their hands out of their pockets and rubbed their eyes or their bruised shins, and have asked all round, Where is the plum? we have it in our mouths, have sucked it, and spit the stone out at their feet.

No sooner is one golden plum snatched and carried off, than Fortune, with a good-humoured smile, attaches another to her thread, and lets it down through the clear air into our midst. What a busy, swarming world ours is, and all the millions that run about are looking for the plums in the wrong places. It is said that the safest place in a thunder-storm is a spot where lightning has already fallen, because it is ten thousand chances to one against the electric bolt descending in the same place again. With Fortune's plums we may be sure that the un-likeliest corner in which to come across one is that where a plum has already been let down. No man when he fishes whips the stream pre-cisely where he whipped last. But this is what few consider. The moment one of us has caught and bolted a plum, there is a rush to the spot, and even a scramble for the stone we have thrown away—and see! all the while behind the backs of the scramblers a golden fruit is dangling, and Fortune shakes her sides with laughter to observe the swarm tossing and heading at the sucked stone, whilst a single knowing one quietly comes up and takes her newly offered plum. The eyes of all the rest are turned in the opposite direction till the opportunity is lost.

In this chapter I am going to relate how Richard Cable caught sight of and got hold of one of Fortune's golden plums; not, indeed, a very large one, but one large enough to satisfy his requirements. It came about in the simplest way, and it came about also in the way least expected.

'Hullooh!'

Whilst Cable was breaking stones on the roadside, Jacob Corye stood before him. He had not seen the host of the 'Magpie' since he had left his roof, nearly a year ago. Since his departure, Richard had occasionally spoken to his mother about Corye, and had told her that the sufferings he had undergone from the weariful talk of the landlord had almost equalled those he endured from his injured thigh. Now that he heard the saw-like voice of Jacob, he looked up and answered ungraciously. He was ill-pleased to renew acquaintance with the man, and be subjected again to his tedious prosing about the rearing and raising and fattening of young stock. Yet that moment was a critical one; on it hung Richard's fortune. Jacob himself had caught a glimpse of the golden plum, and with rare generosity, or rather with by no means singular stupidity, was about to put it into Richard Cable's mouth, and Richard was like a child offered a rare fruit, that bites cautiously, and turns the piece about in the mouth, considering its flavour, and then, at once, having satisfied itself that the quality is excellent, takes the plum at a gulp.

'Hullooh!' said Jacob Corye, standing before Richard, with his hands in his pockets and his legs wide apart, with a pipe in his mouth, and speaking with difficulty and indistinctly because of the pipe, which he was too lazy to remove. 'How be you a-getting on in the world, eh? I needn't ask that, cap'n, when I seez you come down to stone-knacking for a living.'

'If you see that, why do you ask?' inquired Cable irritably.

Jacob continued, imperturbably: 'I reckon you're a bit disappointed with your house. The garden ain't much for the raising and fattening of seven little maids.'

Richard did not answer. He frowned and continued hammering.

'I reckon you're pretty well on wi' the stone-breaking,' said Corye. 'What'll you be on to next?'

'Whatever turns up,' replied Cable curtly.

'That's just it,' the host of the 'Magpie' said; 'and I've come here to look you up and make you an offer. I've been a-troubling and a-worriting my head ever since I came to think at all, about the rearing and the raising of young stock, and how to get rid of the regraders' profits. I don't mean to get rid of 'em either; I mean to get the profits for myself

and do without the regraders. Well, cap'n,
I've figured it out on a bit o' paper. I couldn't
get my ideas into order no other way. Doy'
look here. There's manganese in St. Kerian,
ain't there?'

'Yes,' answered Cable. 'You can see that
for yourself.'

'So I have. I seed the washing-floors, and
the water running red as riddam [ferruginous
water] away from them. There be three or
four washing-floors, ain't there?'

'Yes. You can count them if you are
curious; I am not.'

'Oh, I've nothing to do wi' manganese,'
continued Jacob, 'more than this—that my
meaning is, just as the manganese has to be
washed in this tank, and then in thicky [that
one], and every time it is washed you get rid of
the rummage and get more o' the metal, so is
it with ideas. I've got an idea or two in my
head, and I've been a-stirring and a-scouring of
it over and over for years; but I can't get rid
o' the rummage; there must be another floor
on which to give it a second wash before we
get at the pure metal. So my meaning is, I
want you to take into consideration what I've
a-said about the raising and rearing and fattening of young stock, and give it a second wash
in your brain; and then, I reckon, something'll

come of it. It be them darned regraders as
has to be got rid of—washed out of the cattle,
so to speak.'

'Go on,' said Richard. He knew his man
—that there would be no getting rid of him
till he had talked himself out.

'Doy' look here,' continued Jacob, leisurely
taking one hand out of his pocket, tapping the
ashes from his pipe, replacing his pipe between
his lips, in the corner of his mouth, and then
his hand in his pocket. 'When one of the
quarriers or masons goes on to the tors after
granite, it ain't every piece as will serve his
purpose. He may spend a day over what
seems a fitty [fitting] piece; and then may
discover, when he's half cut it, that it's beddy
[liable to split], or so full of horseteeth [spar]
that he can make nothing out of it, and all his
labour is thrown away. Now, I want you to
lay hold of my idea, and turn it out with a
crowbar from where it lies in the bog—that is,
my head—and split it up and see whether it is
beddy or horsetoothy, or whether there's good
stuff in it for use. I can't do it myself; I've
not had the education. I can show you a score
of ideas bogged in my brains; but I can't tell
you whether they're workable and shapeable.
Now, I ax you to do that; and I'll send you a
kilderkin of " Magpie " ale for your trouble, if

you can find what is usable in my ideas; and, for a beginning, the rearing, and the raising, and the fattening of young cattle.'

'I should have supposed that was the only idea in the bog you call your intellect.'

'There, you're wrong,' said Corye, by no means affronted. 'It is the most remarkable and conspicuous idea, that's all. My mind is like Carnvean Moor. If you go over it, you see the Long Man, a great old ancient stone about twenty feet high, standing upright, that they tell was an idol in the times of the Romans [that is, Roman Catholics]. When you go over the moor, you can see nought but the Long Man; but blow you! doy' suppose there be no more granite there than thicky great stone? If it were took away, you'd find scores on scores of pieces lying about, more than half covered wi' peat and furze and heather.'

'Go on, then, with your Long Man.'

'I'm a-going along as quick as I can; but I can't go faster. I've the pipe in my mouth.'

Jacob smoked leisurely for some minutes, contemplating Cable, who worked on without regarding him.

'It's all very well saying "Go on," when one has an idea, but it ain't possible. If I hadn't an idea I could gallop. It is just the same with the miller's donkey; when the boys get a sack of flour over the donkey's back, the donkey goes at a walk and cautiously. What doy' mean by hollering "Go on!" to him then? He can't gallop his donkey, because of the sack o' flour across it. So is it with me. I must go along quietly and cautiously, at a footpace, because I've got this idea over the back of my intellect; if there were none there, I'd go on at a gallop.'

'Then go on at your own pace,' said Cable, 'and don't zigzag.'

Richard sat breaking the stones and listening at first inattentively to the prosing of the host of the 'Magpie;' but little by little his interest was aroused, and when it was, then he forgot his work. The breaking of the stones became less vigorous, till at last Richard sat looking dreamily before him with the haft of the hammer in his hands and the head resting on a stone. He no more rose the hammer over the stones that day, but hobbled home in a brown study. The thoughts of Jacob Corye, when washed on the floor of his brain, proved to be sterling metal; or, to take another of the landlord's similes, the Long Man of his boggy mind when chipped by Cable's tool proved to be sound stone.

I need not give my readers the turbid talk of Jacob for them to wash, but will let them have the scheme of the innkeeper after it had been sifted and arranged by Cable.

St. Kerian lies eleven miles from Launceston, which is its nearest town. Thither the farmers have to drive their bullocks and sheep for sale. It is even worse for those near the coast; they have to send them some fifteen or twenty miles. At Launceston market the cattle are sold to jobbers, who drive them along the great highroad called Old Street—ancient, no doubt, in Roman times—to Exeter, a distance of thirty-eight or forty miles, where they are resold to dealers from Somersetshire, Gloucestershire, and even Berkshire. Of late years the South-Western line has run to Plymouth by Exeter and Okehampton, so that cattle have been trucked at Lydford, Bridestowe, or Okehampton. Quite recently, in 1886, the South-Western has carried a line into Launceston; but at the time of which I write, the line had not come nearer than Exeter, thirty-eight miles from Launceston, and fifty from St. Kerian, and some sixty from the coast.

Now, Jacob Corye had picked up scraps of information from the coastguard, some of whom came from Gloucestershire and Somersetshire. From them he learned that the farming done there was dairy-farming. Butter and cheese were made and sold at Bath, Bristol, and in

London. The land was good, the pastures rich: no stock was raised there—it did not pay to raise stock, or it did not pay so well as dairy-farming. Along the north coast of Cornwall the land was poor, and exposed to the western sea-gales. Only in the bottoms of the valleys was good pasture and rich alluvial soil. There was a great deal of white clay about, lying in bars from east to west on the hillsides, sometimes filling the valley bottoms; and where that was, nothing would grow but scant grass and rushes, and sheep put on it were certain to rot. This land did well enough for young stock, and was worth from five to ten shillings an acre; but it was fit for nothing else. Corye considered that when the farmers sold their cattle at Launceston, the jobbers who drove them to Okehampton or to Exeter and resold them made a tidy profit; so did the dealers who bought them at Okehampton or Exeter and trucked them on into Somerset, or Gloucester, or Berks. There were at least two profits made out of the bullocks and heifers before they reached their ultimate destination.

Then, again, the dairy-farmers, after that their cows had calved, wanted to get rid of the calves; it did not pay them to rear them on their dairy-land. On the other hand, the North Cornish farmers could not get calves enough to rear on their poor land. When it came to fattening the young stock, they could not do it; they had not good pasturage for that; therefore, they were forced to sell, and sell cheap. In precisely the same manner, the farmers in the dairy counties sold their calves cheap. The bullocks they did not want at all, and the heifers they wanted after they were grown into cows, but not before. So sometimes calves from Somerset travelled down into Cornwall, and travelled back again, after a lapse of a couple of years, into Somerset; and as they went down, they passed through two or three dealers' hands, leaving coin in their several palms; and as they went up, they passed through the same hands, and again left coin in their several palms.

Now Corye saw this confusedly. He had tried his utmost to clear the matter by using a stump of a pencil and a bit of paper, but had only succeeded in further bewildering himself. Cable saw his way at once. There flashed on his eyes the gold of the plum, and he put out his hand for it. He did not take long to consider. He at once offered Corye to drive his stock to Exeter, to truck them there, and go up country with them, and dispose of them in Somersetshire or Gloucestershire. By this means he would save the profits of at least two intermediaries. He proposed that one of these profits should go to Corye, the other to himself. Jacob Corye was to provide him with a cob on which to ride, and was to advance him a small · sum sufficient for the maintenance of his children during his absence. Whatever Corye advanced to him, he was to deduct from Cable's share of the profits on his return. The scheme was so simple and practicable that the host of the 'Magpie' closed with the offer at once. It was a relief to him to find that his ideas were being put into practical shape. This pleased him more than the prospect of making money.

'You see,' said he, shaking hands again and again with Cable, 'I've ideas, but they're bogged.'

'Do more,' said Richard, 'than send your own stock; buy of your neighbours, that I may have a large drove. The larger the drove, so long as it is manageable, the more the money that will come in.'

'Doy' look here,' said Jacob. 'I'm a liberal man wi' them as deals liberal wi' me. I'll keep all your little maids on "Magpie" ale as long as you're away, and no charge. I said a kilderkin, I say two.'

'Thank you,' answered Richard. 'The little girls drink only water and milk.'

Cable finished the work he had to do for

the waywardens on the road ; he said nothing to anyone in St. Kerian, except his mother, about his projected journey ; but he went over to the ' Magpie' once before starting, to concert plans, and see a coastguardman who came out of Somersetshire, and who, Corye thought, might be of use to him. The man was anxious to send a message home, and with the message some Cornish crystals set in bog oak as a brooch for his sister, who kept an inn near Bath ; also some specimens of peacock copper, and spar with tin ore in it, and mundic. These samples of the riches of Cornwall would interest the Somersetshire folk of his native village of Bewdley. Cable took the names of some of the farmers about the place, and promised to lodge at the inn and give the specimens and the brooch.

' My sister,' said the coastguardman, ' has a lot o' little childer.'

' Very well,' said Richard. ' I'm certain to put up with her. What is her inn ? '

' The " Otterbourne Arms." It belongs to an old lady who is squiress of the place, called Otterbourne.'

Richard received his instructions from Jacob ; they were confused and unintelligible. He almost offended him and brought the agreement to a condition of rupture by declining ' Magpie' beer.

'I've a notion of taking the pledge,' he said.

'More's the reason you should drink now, afore you does,' argued Corye.

The night before his departure, Richard Cable could not sleep. He saw that the golden plum was let down within his reach, and he had his hand on it. There remained to him only to bite into the rich fruit. But in this case, as in all other in this world, every good thing brings with it something bad—there is no gain without loss. If he were about to rise from want to plenty, he must consent to be much parted from his children. What this meant to him, few can understand. We all have our interests, our friends, our studies, and although we love our children, they do not engross our whole thoughts, occupy our hearts to the exclusion of everything else. With Richard Cable it was otherwise. He had no friends, no acquaintances, no pursuits, no interests apart from his children. He lived for nothing else, he thought of nothing else. He worked for nothing else; he loved nothing else, except his mother. The wrench to him was almost unendurable. He had given up the thought of going to sea after his accident, because he could not bear to be parted from them; and now he only left them because he had resolved to make his dream come true, and in no other way that he could see was that dream to be realised.

Richard kept a little lamp alight all the night before he left home, because he left his bed every hour to look at one after another of the seven little sleeping heads, and to wonder which he could best spare, should it please that sullen Providence, which so ill-used him, to take one away whilst he was absent. He found that he could not part with dearest Mary, so thoughtful and forbearing with others, so full of love and kindness to the younger ones —so like a little mother to them, though she was only fourteen years old; nor with Effie, so sprightly, with her twinkling eyes, and that dimple in her ever-laughing cheek; nor with Jane, who clung to Effie, being her twin-sister, and who must go if Effie went; nor with Martha, who had such endearing, coaxing ways; nor with Lettice, with a voice like a lark, so shrill, yet withal so clear and sweet; nor with Susie the pickle, who already knew her letters, and could say BA—Ba, and one and two makes three; no—she said BA spells sheep, and one and two makes four; no, not with Bessie the baby, Bessie, whom after all it would be best that God should take.—No, no, no—ten thousand times no!

# CHAPTER XLIII.

## A LOW LOT.

WHEN the morning broke, Richard Cable did not dare to kiss the white brows or the rosy cheeks of his sleeping children; but he took little locks of their shining hair between his fingers and put his lips to them, and dropped over each alike a clear tear-drop, and then went away before the seven pairs of bright eyes opened, and the little voices began to chirp and laugh and chatter.

Richard Cable drove his herd of young cattle all the way from St. Kerian to Exeter, some fifty miles. There he trucked them on the Bristol and Exeter line, and travelled with them into Somersetshire, where he disposed of them to such advantage that he was well content. But he would not return with only money in his pocket. He had a van constructed, very light, on four wheels, for his cob, and he bought as many calves, a week or ten days old, as he could convey in this van.

He made Bewdley his headquarters, and
stayed at the 'Otterbourne Arms,' where was
the landlady, Mrs. Stokes, the sister of the
coastguardman at Pentargon. To her he re-
mitted the spar, and the mundic, and the
brooch of bog-oak with Cornish crystals in it.
She was a tidy, red-cheeked woman, with
many children.

Cable was a temperate man. He remembered that terrible night when he let little
Bessie fall. He never got that experience out
of his mind; consequently, he was on his guard
against the temptations of a cattle-jobber's life
—the sealing of every bargain with a drink.
So he drank cold toast-and-water when he
could, but he had taken no pledge. 'What's
the good of a pledge to me?' he asked himself.
'I've only to think of Bessie's back, and if I
had the best spirits in the world before me,
I would not touch it.'

'Have you any relatives this way?' asked
Mrs. Stokes one Saturday evening. 'There's a
young woman of your name at the Hall, a
lady's-maid to Miss Otterbourne.'

'I have no relatives,' answered Richard,
'but the seven and my mother who are under
my roof at St. Kerian, in Cornwall.'

''Tis a curious and outlandish sort of a
name, too,' said Mrs. Stokes. 'I mean, it ain't

a name one expects to come across twice in a lifetime.'

Richard shrugged his shoulders.

'Here comes Mr. Polkinghorn the footman,' said the landlady. 'He does come here at times to see if there be any one to have a talk with. He can tell you all about your namesake.'

'I am not interested about her,' answered Richard. 'I have none that belong to me save the seven and my mother, and they—I know where they are, under my own roof.'

'Good-evening, Mr. Polkinghorn; how do you find yourself?—And how is Miss Otterbourne?'

'We are both of us pretty well. She's been suffering a little from nettlerash, that has made her fractious, and she has rung the bell outrageous; but she's better now, and I'm middling, thank you. Worreted with her nettlerash and the constant ringing of the bell caused by the irritation. First, it was the blinds were not drawn to her fancy; then it was she wanted a lump of coal with the wood in the grate; and then the venetian blinds must come down, or be turned, or pulled up; and then the geranium or pelargonium on the table—I'm blessed, Mrs. Stokes, if I know what is the difference between a geranium and a pelargonium—wanted water;

or she desired another book from the library. It really is wonderful, Mrs. Stokes—I'll have a glass of beer, thank you—how a little matter upsets a whole household. It comes of lobster mayonaise or cucumber, one or t'other, which don't agree with the old woman. If she takes either of them and she's roaring fond of them, she gets eruptions, generally nettlerash ; and when she's got eruptions, it disturbs us all, keeps the whole household capering : one has to go for the doctor, another has to get cooling fomentations, and her temper is that awful, it is a wonder we stand it. But we know her, and put it down to disorder of the system. We must bear and forbear ; must we not, Mrs. Stokes ? so we pass over all the aggravations, as good Christians and philanthropists.'

'You've not been introduced,' said the hostess. 'You don't know this gentleman, Mr. Cable of Cornwall.'

'Cornwall !' exclaimed the footman. 'You don't happen to have come across the manor and mansion of Polkinghorn anywhere thereabouts, do you ? Our family come from the West of England, and have a lordship called after us ; but I don't exactly know where it is. Still, it's traditional in the family that there is one. We've come down in life ; but so have many great folks ; and lord ! sir—what are our

British aristocracy now? Mushrooms, sir, creatures of to-day. Bankers and brewers and civil engineers, who were not even known, who had not lifted their heads out of the dust, when the Polkinghorns were lords of manors and drove their coach-and-four.'

Mrs. Stokes produced the ale.

'I'll take a mouthful of bread and cheese with it,' said the footman, who was not now in livery.—' So you, sir, are called Cable. We've a Cable among us.'

'Do you mean among the Polkinghorns?'

'Polkinghorns, sir!' said the footman, bridling up. 'I do not, sir, think such a name as Cable has found its way among us, into our tree, sir. I alluded to an inmate of the Hall, sir, a lady's-maid there, who is a Rope or a Cable, or something of that sort— possibly, as she is not stout, merely a twine.' Then as he finished his glass of ale: 'Excuse my freedom, sir; I am generally accounted a wit. I once sent a trifle to *Punch*.'

'Was it inserted?'

'I sent it, sir; that suffices. I do not myself suppose that our Cable does belong to you. There is a lack of style—a want of finish—you understand me, which proclaims inferiority. Not bad-looking, either, is Miss Josephine.'

'What!' shouted Cable, springing to his feet and striking the table. 'What did you say?'

Mr. Polkinghorn stared at him and backed his chair from the table. He did not like the expression on the stranger's face; he thought the man might be a lunatic; therefore, with great presence of mind, he drew the cheese-knife from his plate and secreted it in the pocket of his short coat.

'I asked you a question,' cried Richard. 'What did you say?'

'Merely, dear sir, merely that—that we have a lady's-maid attending on our old woman who is good-looking, but wanting in what I should consider—breeding. If she be a relative, I am sorry——'

'What is her name?'

'Josephine Cable.'

'How long has she been with you?'

'Since last September. She was well recommended; she brought excellent testimonials. Her character quite irreproachable—from some good friends of ours, the Sellwoods of Essex, a respectable family, unfortunate in having gone into the Church. I should have preferred the Army for them.'

'Why is she——' Cable stopped; he was trembling. He put his hand to the table to steady himself. 'I mean—who is she?'

'I do not know,' answered Mr. Polkinghorn.
'She is uncommunicative; that is what I mean
when I say she has not the breed of a lady.
She ain't at her ease and familiar with us. She
is reserved, as she might call it; awkward, as I
should say. If we ask her questions, she don't
answer. She's maybe frightened at finding herself in such high society; and I'm not surprised.
I don't fancy she was in other than a third-class
situation before—with some people in business
or profession—not real aristocrats. That does
make a person feel out of her element when she
rises to our walk of life. It is just the same as
if you were to invite a common sailor to a din-
ner-party among millionaires and aristocrats—
how would he feel? He'd look this way and
that and be without power of speech. He
wouldn't know where to put his feet and how
to behave himself. It is much the same with
Miss Cable. She's not been brought up to our
line of life, and don't understand it, and is as
miserable among us as a common sailor would
be among gentlemen and ladies.'

'Did you say *Miss* Cable?'

'To be sure I did. I don't suppose she's a
married woman. She wears no gold wedding
ring.'

'And her Christian name is—— ?'

'Josephine. But then we always call her

Miss Cable, and our old woman calls her Cable.'

'She has never said a word to you of her family?'

'Not a word. Better not, I suspect. I don't fancy there's anything very high about it. Judging by her manners, I should say she was —excuse my saying it—a low lot.'

'Nor whence she comes?'

'Mum as a mummy—excuse the joke. I am said to be witty. Humour runs in the Polkinghorn blood.'

'Nor what brought her to take service?'

'Necessity—of course. No lady would so demean herself unless forced.—Will you take a glass of ale with me?'

'With pleasure,' answered Cable; 'and I'll ask you not to mention my name at your place —not to the young lady you speak of.'

'I understand,' said Mr. Polkinghorn with a wink and a tap of his nose with his finger. 'Poor relations are nuisances; they come a-sucking and a-sponging, and are a drag on a man who is making his way. No, sir, I'll not say a word.—May I ask if she *is* a relative?'

'I have not seen her. I cannot say.'

'Does the name Josephine run in the family, as John Thomas does in that of Polkinghorn?'

'We never had one baptised by that name.'

'I myself,' said the footman, 'intend to marry some day, so as to perpetuate John Thomas. I'm not sure that I may not take Miss Raffles. I won't deny that I had a tenderness towards the Cable at first; she is good-looking, has fine eyes, splendid hair; a brunette, you understand, with olive skin, and such a figure! But I could not stand the want of polish and ease which go with the true lady, and that she will never get among us.'

Richard left the room abruptly. He was greatly moved, partly with surprise at finding Josephine in such a position, partly with anger at the insolence of the footman.

This latter looked after him contemptuously. 'Well, Mrs. Stokes,' he said, 'I've only come on two Cables in the course of my experience, and, dash me, if there be not a twist in them both.'

Richard went forth, and did not return to the inn till late. He walked by the river. He was disturbed in mind. Mr. Sellwood had told him nothing of Josephine's plan of going into service; he had not felt himself authorised to do this; and at the time he saw Cable, he doubted whether Josephine's resolution might not be overcome. All that Cable knew was that she had surrendered the estate and left the Hall. She was proud, and would have nothing to do

with a property that came to her, as she con-
cluded, unjustly; and he was proud, he would
accept no property that was offered to him by
her. But that she had been so reduced in circumstances by this voluntary surrender as to
oblige her to earn her bread by menial work,
seemed to him impossible. Her father was a
man of some fortune. It was not possible that
he would consent to her leaving him for such a
purpose. Yet how else could he account for
Josephine's being at Bewdley Manor in the
capacity represented?

There was a mistake. This could not be
she. Some one else was in the house who had
assumed her name. He could not be satisfied
till he had seen her. But he would not allow
himself to be seen by her. He hobbled along
the river-path leaning on his stick, racking his
brain over the questions that arose, seeking
solutions which always escaped him. To whom
at Hanford could he apply for information concerning the affairs and movements of his wife?
There was no one but Mr. Sellwood, and to
him he would not write. His brother-in-law,
Jonas Flinders, was dead, and he shrank from
corresponding on the subject with any of his
old mates.

Then he suddenly burst into a bitter laugh.
Was this his Josephine, this servant-girl, whom

the vulgar flunky, and with him her fellow-
servants, despised as not up to their level,
wanting in style—a low lot? Josephine, who
had scorned his lack of breeding, was herself
looked down on by the ignoble tribe of pariahs
on civilisation! It was a just judgment on
her. How she must toss and writhe, what
agonies of rage and humiliation she must endure in such association! 'A low lot!' shouted
Cable, slashing at the bulrush-heads on the
bank, and laughed savagely—'a low lot!'
But then a gentler feeling came over him, a
wave of his old kindliness and pity, so long
suppressed or beaten back. He saw his
haughty, splendid, wilful Josephine surrounded
by these common-minded, swaggering, vain, un-
intelligent, and debased creatures—alone, cold,
stern, eating out her heart rather than show
her disgust and shame. If it had been misery
to him to be transferred to a condition of life
above him to which he was unfitted, it must
be misery to her to be flung down into a
sphere to her infinitely distasteful and repellent.
He was a man, who could hold his own or
retire with dignity. She was a girl, helpless.
His heart began to flutter, and he turned his
steps into the path by a wicket gate. The
evening was still, the sky clear. The great
trees stood against the silver-gray sky as blots.

The dew was falling heavily ; the grass was charged with water. He might as well have been wading in a stream as walking through it. So heavily was the dew falling that the leaves of the trees were laden with the moisture, and bowed under the weight, and dripped as with rain. The glowworms shone in the damp banks and among the grass under the tree trunks. The stars were twinkling in the sky, looking golden in contrast with the bluish light of the glowworms ; an auroral haze hung over the set sun, fringed with a faint tinge of ruddy brown before it died into the deep gray blue of the night-sky.

He drew near to the house, and a watchdog in the back court began to bark. It had heard his steps on the gravel of the drive. Richard stepped off the carriage-way upon the turf and remained still. The dog hearing no further noise presently desisted from barking. Then Richard moved on through the grass till he came where he could see the front of Bewdley Manor-house. Three tall windows were lighted, one somewhat brilliantly, the next less so, the third least of all. It was clear that all three belonged to one room, perhaps a drawing-room, and that the lamp that illumined it was at one end. The window which was at the further end was half open, the blind was drawn up, and Richard could make out gilt frames to large pictures on a dark wall. He stood, looking at the three windows, wondering whether a shadow would pass, and by the shadow he could tell who it was that passed. Did he desire to see Josephine again? He shrank from so doing; but he was uneasy at the thought that she was in this great house a servant, with fellows like Polkinghorn about her. As he stood thus looking up, he heard the notes of a piano issue from the open window. The first chords that were struck made him start and a shiver pass through his limbs. Then he heard a clear voice, rich and sweet, sing:

> O wie wogt es sich schön auf der Fluth
> Wenn die müde Well im Schlummer ruht!

It was the familiar song from *Oberon*. When Richard heard this, he put his hands to his ears to shut out the sound, and ran as hard as he could run with his faulty thigh along the road; and the dog heard his retreating steps and barked furiously. Cable heeded nothing, but ran on, with the sweat breaking out on his brow and dripping from his face, as it had dripped on that night when he ran to Brentwood Hall, and as now the dew was dripping from the leaves of the trees in the park. Only when he

reached the river-bank outside the park gate,
away from the sight of the house and the
sound of the song, did he halt and strike his
stick angrily, passionately, into the oozy soil,
and cry out, half sobbingly, half savagely : ' A
low lot !  A low lot ! '

# CHAPTER XLIV.

### A ROLLING STONE.

RICHARD CABLE started homewards. He had ridden his cob to Exeter, and brought him on thence with the cattle by train. Now he drove him all the way back from Somersetshire to St. Kerian, but not with the van full of calves the whole way, for he sold them all before he had reached Launceston. Then, instead of going on, he bought up young cattle in Devon, to the north of the road, where is also a wide tract of very poor clay soil, worthless except for rearing stock. In the north of Devon the soil varies to such an extent, that one field may let for five times the price of the field next to it. Where the red soil runs, there anything will grow; where the white clay lies, there nothing will thrive. Now, after the old Roman road from Exeter to Launceston passes North Tawton, it leaves the red soil for ever. On the south of the road is good land—crops wave, and trees grow to stately dimensions; for there limestone

and volcanic tufa break out and warm and
enrich the soil above. To the north of the
road is clay, and clay only, to the ocean, where
crops are meagre and trees are stunted. Cable's
eye had been sharpened, and he learned and
took in much as he went along the road.
Having bought young stock from the poor
land, he turned his back on the west, and drove
them to Exeter, and trucked them on to Somersetshire again; but not this time to Bewdley
and Bath, but to the neighbourhood of Wells.
He sold these readily enough; and then he
bought more calves and trucked them to
Exeter, where on this occasion he had left his
cob and van; and then drove them to Launceston, disposing of most of them before reaching home.

From Exeter he brought with him seven
pairs of new shoes, with perfectly clean smooth
soles, of a pleasant brown; and ever and anon,
as he drove in his van, with the calves bleating
behind him, he opened the bag that contained
the shoes, and took them out and counted
them, and kissed the soles, thinking of the little
feet they would clothe when brought to St.
Kerian. Richard had to halt continually on
the road and buy milk for his calves, dip his
fingers in the milk and let the calves suck
them. It was tedious work; but it would have

been less tedious to another, for no other was drawn homewards by such strong fibres from his heart. At length he arrived within sight of St. Kerian, and drove through the village street. The innkeeper came out to ask what luck he had had. 'Middling,' answered Dick; but he did not halt at the inn-door. Then out of his smithy came Penrose, the blacksmith, with a cheery salute and his big black hand extended.

'Well, Cable, glad to see y' back. The little 'uns be all peart [bright].'

Richard nodded. He held the reins in one hand and the whip in the other; he did not accept the offered hand, but drove on.

'What, Mr. Cable!' exclaimed the parson, who was on his rounds. 'You're home again! I'm glad to see you have a carriage. Your mother is fairly well, and the children—blooming rosebuds.'

'Thanky', sir!' Richard put the handle of his whip to his cap, and drove on.

'Dicky!' shouted Farmer Tregurtha over the hedge, 'so you're home with your pockets lined with money. I must look out for Summerleaze, or you'll snap it away from under my feet.'

'I take nothing for which I cannot pay,' answered Richard; then he turned a corner and stopped the van, whereat the calves, thinking it meant milk and a suck at his hands, began to bleat. But he was not thinking at that moment of the calves. He saw before him the cob cottage, the limewashed walls gleaming white in the sun, and before the door stood Mrs. Cable with little Bessie in her arms, and about her the rest, looking down the road with eager eyes.

What a happy evening that was, with his children clustering round the calves, dipping their hands in the milk and laughing, but first shrinking at the mouths of the young creatures sucking their hands. Little Bessie must pat the calves, and she quite fell in love with a young dappled Guernsey. What a pleasant supper when they all sat round the table, but not before there had been a slight scuffle which should sit beside their father. Was there ever so dainty a dish served up at Hanford Hall whilst Richard dined there, as that great bowl of potatoes and turnips that now steamed in the midst of the table round which the bright and happy faces smiled and shone! Then, when supper was over, came the trying on of the new shoes; and each in turn sat on her grandmother's lap, whilst Richard knelt on the slate floor and fitted the covers on to the dear little feet he loved so well. For Bessie there was a pair of glazed patent leather that shone like sticking-plaster, and they had rosettes with steel buckles and beads over the instep. Bessie laughed and danced in her grandmother's arms, and then cried to be held by her dada; and clung fast to him, and would not be put down, or go to bed till he undertook to undress her, wash her, comb her hair, hear her prayers, and sit by her till she fell asleep.

The happiness was of short duration. Next morning, Richard went farther with his van and cob and calves, to the 'Magpie,' to give an account of what he had done, how he had succeeded, and what he proposed to do, to Jacob Corye.

'There, now,' said the landlord of the 'Magpie,' when he heard the results and saw his money, ' I be glad, I be, to handle the cash; but I be main better pleased to know that what some say are the maggots in my head have turned into butterflies, and not blue-bottles.'

After that, of course a second venture was agreed upon. Richard was to remain a week at home, make what arrangements he thought necessary for the children, and then start again on the road by Launceston to Exeter, driving young cattle before him. He was now eager to be gone. Not that he desired to be away from his family, but that his ambition was fired. He was resolved at no very distant date to secure Summerleaze, and build thereon the house which he had seen in a dream.

Throughout the week he was at home Richard was silent concerning one matter. He was ready to talk to his little ones about what he had seen—concerning the children of Mrs. Stokes, the whirligig he had come across at Okehampton, and the grand cathedral at Exeter, and the piebald horses of a circus that had passed him on the road, and the militia reviewed at Wells, and the hot springs with foul smell at Bath; and he had told his mother of his difficulties and of his successes, of his mistakes and of his gained experiences, of his prospects for the future, of the certainty of his insuring a small fortune; but he said not a word about the discovery he had made at Bewdley. Nevertheless, that discovery troubled his mind and kept him wakeful at night. It was a discovery that perplexed him beyond power of setting to rights. Why was Josephine in service? If in service, how came she to be singing and playing in the drawing-room that night? He knew so much of the ways of good houses as this, that a lady's-maid is not expected to sit down to the piano in the room with her mistress. He also knew so much of Josephine as this, that for her to associate with such creatures as Mr. Polkinghorn would be unendurable. He thought of his own Polly; perhaps the maids at Bewdley were like her. Polly was a good girl, fond of work, and fond also of finery when she could get it. Polly had not been blessed by heaven with much mind, and what little mind she had was uncultivated. She could read, but read only trash—police intelligence and novels. She could write, but not spell. She could talk, but not of anything beyond village gossip. Could Josephine have borne the daily society of Polly, could she breathe in such an atmosphere of vulgar interests?

Either Josephine was very much other than what he had supposed, or she was now completely out of her proper element, and suffering accordingly. It was possible that her pride, her headlong self-will, coupled with pride, had made her throw up all the advantages she had got by the will of Gabriel Gotham. Richard recollected now that she had told him her mother's fortune, which ought to have come to her, had been mismanaged and lost. It was by no means impossible that Mr. Cornellis, for whom Richard entertained the greatest aversion, might have met with a reverse and be ruined. Then how was it that Josephine, being so close a friend of the Sellwoods, was allowed by them to drop into a menial situation? They were

well off, always ready to do what was kind,
and be helpful to those in distress. Yet it was
the Sellwoods who, according to Mr. Polkinghorn, had recommended Josephine to her
present place.

'I wish I could have seen her,' mused
Richard. 'It would be painful to me—but for
all that, I wish I had seen her; and when I go
back again to Bewdley, I must try and see her
without letting her see me. I'd like to know
how she bears the change. I'd like to see how
she looks—as a servant.' He laughed. 'And
to be considered a low lot!'

Dicky Cable did not go near Bath on his
second expedition; he went into another part
of Somerset. He was away for some time.
After this he was able to stand unsupported by
Jacob Corye. He became a cattle-jobber on
his own bottom; but he always dealt for Corye
whilst dealing for himself, and to Corye he
always gave double profits, for it was the landlord of the 'Magpie' who had put the plum into
his mouth. He began to turn over money very
fast. He had a good deal of expense on his
journeys: he had to lodge himself and his
horse, and feed his young stock and give
skimmed milk to his calves; and the railway
carriage ran away with money; and the seven
little mouths at home cost more every day, for

appetites grew with their bodies, and their clothing and shoeing cost more also. Nevertheless, Cable put away money.

But we are looking too far ahead. He had not started on his own foundation when Christmas came ; he did so with the New Year.

The opinions of the St. Kerian people underwent a change respecting him. Some were glad at the improvement in his circumstances ; but others begrudged it. Most wondered that he should have done what was now obvious to all ; they were uneasy at his having got his feet on Luck's road, when there were so many worthier men, such as themselves, who wandered in Poverty Lane. Now, those who formerly had not noticed him, nodded when he passed ; and those who in former days had nodded shook hands ; and those who had in the time when he broke stones shaken hands, now asked him to lend them money, which was the greatest mark of esteem they could show him. The St. Kerian folk were in that transition mood in which it would take very little on his part to bring them into the most cordial relationship, and make them forget that on one side he was not a true-blooded Cornishman. The women were specially disposed in his favour, because he had proved himself so tender and. true a father to his orphan girls ; and some were most especially so disposed because they considered him to be a widower. But Richard Cable took no notice of the revolution. He called at none of the houses of the villagers; he scarcely spoke to those whom he passed; he returned their salutations without cordiality; and he never went to the public-house, which was the more to be marvelled at, because, whilst from home, he lived entirely in taverns. Perhaps that was why he cared for none when at St. Kerian, and spent all his available time in his cob cottage among his seven little maids.

Christmas came—the second since Richard Cable and his family had been at St. Kerian. The first saw him in great poverty, without prospect of betterment; the second shone on him with a future opening before him; but it did not find him, for all that, with a more softened and Christmas-like spirit. He arrived at home on the eve.

Over the great fire that burned on what is locally termed the 'heath-grate' hung a caldron, in which was boiling the plum-pudding for the morrow. Cable sat in the armchair by the fire, with little Bessie on one knee and Susie on the other with Lettice standing in the chair behind him, scrambling up his back, and the four other children sitting on their stools in a semicircle round the fire.

They were in neat stuff frocks, with clean white pinafores over them. The father was full of joy and fun, when a tap came at the door, and some neighbours entered to congratulate him on his return and to hear the news.

They stood before the fire, thrusting the little girls aside, talking, asking questions, hinting pretty broadly their desire to know how his affairs went—well-intentioned visitors, with kindly meant inquiries, but vexing to Cable, who did not care to be disturbed. He answered shortly, with gravity; he showed no pleasure at their visit; he put aside their questions unanswered. He did not ask the intruders to be seated and take a pipe; so that, after a few minutes, somewhat disconcerted, they retired. An opportunity for conciliation had been offered and rejected.

Richard Cable had never cared for the society of his fellow-men, even in the old days, but then he had not shunned it. Now that he had entered on a business which took him among men, he valued his privacy more than formerly. He was not at home for very long, and whilst there he desired to be left alone with his precious ones. The St. Kerian people were not travellers; they remained stationary where their fathers had stood, and their grandfathers before them. Richard Cable had become a rolling stone, after having fallen among them with every promise of becoming a fixture. The proverb says that a rolling stone gathers no moss; but the St. Kerian stones collected very little, and Cable at every roll came back with the gold moss clinging to him. A rolling stone he was, stony to all he encountered, hard, unyielding, but with his centre of gravity never displaced, always drawing him towards the cob cottage; and when he was there, there was nothing stony about him, there he was soft, soft as moss.

Scarce had the visitors gone, when another rap came at the door, and before he had called to enter, the door flew open, and in danced several mummers. St. George, with a tin pot and a cock's feather for helmet and plume, and a fishpan-lid for shield, and a red shawl for mantle; the dragon of pasteboard overlaid with tinfoil. King Herod with a gold-paper crown and corked moustache and beard. Beelzebub with a black sweep's suit and complexion to match. Some of the smallest of the children began to cry—Bessie and Susie, who were on his knees; Lettice stood behind him, peering over his shoulder, feeling herself safe behind such a bulwark; but the others laughed, jumped about like kids, and clapped their hands. Cable would have driven the mummers out; he threatened them; but Mary and Martha interposed and entreated him to let them see the show. Then ensued the old-fashioned masque of St. George and the Dragon in doggerel rhyme. The mummers were all boys, and they had learnt the traditional play by heart. They recited their parts without much animation and action, as though saying their collects in Sunday school. It was dull fun to Cable; but it delighted the little maidens, their delight reaching its climax when Mary cried out: 'Oh! I know who St. George is! You are Walter Penrose.' Thereat St. George interrupted the performance to pull a huge, red-streaked apple, a quarendon, out of his trousers-pocket, and present it to Mary with a bow and a laugh: 'And this is St. George's Christmas present to little Mary Cable.'

Then the demon brandished his club, made of sacking, enclosing hay, and, banging the performers with it right and left, shouted at the top of his voice:

Up and cometh Beelzebub,
And knocketh them all down with his club.

Whereupon the mummers danced out of the door. Then Richard Cable stood up, put down Bessie and Susie, and shook off Lettice, and

went to the door and put the bolt across it
and turned the lock.

'O father!' cried Mary, 'wasn't that kind
of Walter? He is so good! He always gives
me sugar-plums whenever I see him.'

'My dear Mary,' said her father, 'I object
to your receiving any presents from any St.
Kerian people. Walter——. Is he the blacksmith's son? Well, the time will come when
you will hold up your heads too high to take
apples from and play with the sons of common
village blacksmiths. Throw that apple away!'

'O father!' cried all the little girls together.

'Don't say that,' pleaded Mary. 'Take out
your knife, father, and cut the apple into seven.'

'Very well,' he said moodily; 'this time, but
this only. Let it be the last ; and understand,
Mary, that you take nothing again from Walter
Penrose or from any other St. Kerian child.'

'But, papa,' said little Mary, 'Walter is so
kind, and when we get old, I am going to be
his little wife.'

'Never,' said Cable angrily—'never.'

Then, all at once, outside burst forth the
song of the Christmas carollers :

> Hark ! the herald-angels sing
> Glory to the new-born King,
> Peace on earth, and mercy mild,
> God and sinners reconciled.

'But Richard Cable did not open the door and look forth and wish the singers a glad Noël, and offer them plumcake and a jug of cider. In all his children's eyes looking at him was trembling entreaty, but he heeded it not. He sat by the fire, looking gloomily into it.

Then the seven little girls raised their voices, and sang inside the cottage, along with the choir without:

> Joyful, all ye nations rise,
> Join the triumph of the skies ;
> With the angelic host proclaim,
> Christ is born in Bethlehem.

'My children sing better than the trained choristers outside,' said Cable to himself. He sat motionless, though the carollers waited without for their Christmas greeting. They did not get it. The rolling stone was stone indeed ; and the more it rolled, and the more the prospect of gathering gold-moss opened before it, the more flinty it became.

Then the choir went away, and the hushed children and their silent father heard the singers carolling before another house half a mile away. The music came to them faint and sad. There was no peace, no mercy mild and reconciliation in the heart of Richard Cable that Christmas Eve.

# CHAPTER XLV.

### MISS OTTERBOURNE.

JOSEPHINE'S position in Bewdley Manor had gone through a change, a change advantageous in one way, but bringing with it great vexations.

Miss Otterbourne was a small old lady of delicate bones and mind, of small ideas and petty interests. She lived in her great house without a companion, made calls in her grand carriage when the coachman allowed her to use the fat horses, pottered in her conservatories about her flowers, and picked them only when suffered to do so by the head-gardener. She kept a great many servants, and was badly served by them. She spent a great deal of money and had little pleasure out of it. Josephine was shocked to see how the old lady was pillaged by all her attendants. She kept cows, and bought her butter; poultry, and purchased her eggs; had gamekeepers, but ate very little game. Her pheasants cost her about their weight in silver. She grew grapes and apricots and nectarines and peaches, which the gardener sold in Bath, and put the money into his own pocket. Her porcelain was broken, and had to be replaced incessantly, because the china shopkeeper tipped the breakers for every breakage. Every tradesman who attended the house put money into the servants' pockets, on the understanding that they made work for artisans there. Every shopkeeper who dealt with the house gave a percentage to the servants to encourage waste. Coal-waggons were incessantly bringing their loads to the house, which apparently consumed as much as a glass-furnace; but the coal-cellar door was left always open for all the cottagers to supply themselves from it, and a sack was deposited every turn of the waggon at the gardener's, or the gamekeeper's, or at the lodge, or at the coachman's, or at the house of the mother of the boy who cleaned the knives. The gardener was annually carrying off prizes at flower-shows; but the greenhouses were never properly stocked, and fresh supplies, enough to fill every stage, had to be ordered from the nurserymen every autumn and spring. Fifteen hogsheads of ale were got rid of in that house in the twelvemonths, by a household of tee-totalers; the wine cellar needed the laying down of expensive wines every year, although

Miss Otterbourne no longer gave dinner-parties.
A milliner and her assistant from Bath were
engaged in Bewdley House half their time, yet
Miss Otterbourne only had two new gowns in
the year. Bewick's 'British Birds' and 'Fishes'
and 'Quadrupeds' deserted the shelves of the
library, as if they were leaving the Ark of
Noah, and turned up in a second-hand book-
seller's at Bath. Valuable pieces of old Wor-
cester china, fine Chelsea figures, unaccountably
got mislaid; but certain dealers in London
would have been happy to sell them back to
the good lady.

'My servants,' said Miss Otterbourne, 'are
perfectly trusty. I have left my purse about;
I have allowed coppers to remain on my
chimney-piece, and I have never lost a farthing.'

It is a curious fact that the conscience of
many domestic servants draws a line at money,
It is most rare to find one who will purloin a
coin ; but beyond that line, in far too many
cases, all scruple ceases.

Josephine soon discovered how her mistress
was being plundered. The housekeeper winked
at the petty robberies; she shut her eyes to a
good deal more that filled Josephine with horror
and disgust. John Thomas Polkinghorn was
vain and foolish, but he was not vicious.
Among the many men attached to the house

in one capacity or another, he was the most respectable; but the old butler, Vickary, on whom Miss Otterbourne chiefly relied as a trusty servant who had the interests of the family at heart, was a prime source of evil in the place. Josephine made him keep his distance. She behaved towards him with such proud reserve and scarce veiled abhorrence, that he scowled at her and prophesied her speedy dismissal. The other servants, all cringing to the butler, took his tone, and behaved to Josephine with insolence, at least in his presence. Yet, behind his back they were ready to speak to her with kindness, and show her little attentions. They let her understand that they groaned under his tyranny, but were too timorous to revolt. The house was, moreover, too good to be left, except for some extraordinary chance of betterment ; and servants who came there well-intentioned gradually swallowed their scruples and sank to the general level.

That Josephine was not more with them was due to the forethought of Mrs. Sellwood, who wrote confidentially to her sister to tell her that Josephine had known better days, was well educated, and by birth a lady, forced by circumstances she was not at liberty to disclose, to go into menial service. Miss Otterbourne was the kindest-hearted of old maids, a generally

kind-hearted race, but she was weak. She
had fallen a prey to several unscrupulous ladies'-
maids in succession. Girls well recommended
had come to her, and the general bad tone of
the house had lowered them; she herself had
contributed to their deterioration by ill-judged
kindness, by making of them confidantes, and
almost friends. She had trusted them, when
they were neither by education nor character
worthy to be trusted. They had abused her
kindness. One after another had taken to
drink. Miss Otterbourne would not believe it;
she supposed poor Jane or Marianne or Emily
was subject to fits, or had a weak heart; and
Mrs. Sellwood had sometimes to come down from
Essex to rout a disagreeable and disreputable
companion from her sister's house. The old
lady, perhaps feeling her loneliness, and with
her heart craving for love, was so liable to fall
under the dominion of her servants, that Mrs.
Sellwood was glad to be able to assist Josephine
and her own sister at once, to put the former
with one who would be kind to her, and to
give the latter a companion who was perfectly
reliable.

Miss Otterbourne at once perceived that
her new attendant was what her sister had
described her—a lady, and with her natural

kindness, did what lay in her power to soften
to her the hardship of her lot.

On the morning after her arrival at Bewdley, Josephine rose with a weight on her heart.
She had not slept well. She was pale, and her
eyes looked large and sad when she appeared
before Miss Otterbourne to assist her in dressing. The old lady spoke gently to her. She
told her that she had heard from Mrs. Sellwood
that Josephine had met with troubles which had
forced her into a situation for which she was
not born, and assured her that she would be a
good mistress to her, and not exact from her
more than was really needed.

'My servants are all so honest and so respectable, and so devoted to me, that I am sure
you will like them. They never give me any
trouble, and set a good example to the entire
parish. But as you belong by birth to a
superior class, you will not mix with them
much. I shall expect you to be chiefly about
my person, and when not engaged in dressing
me to attend to my wardrobe. I should be
glad if you could read to me in the evenings.
I cannot use my eyes by lamplight—at least
not much, and the evenings are tedious to me.
I play patience, but one tires in time even of
patience.'

Later on Miss Otterbourne made overtures

to get into Josephine's confidence, but without
avail. Josephine's secret was not one she cared
to share. She soon fell into her work ; it was
not difficult, and the old lady was not exacting.
She felt how considerate towards her Miss
Otterbourne was, and she was grateful for it,
but not inclined to open her heart to her.
Miss Otterbourne was not one who could understand her course of conduct or appreciate her
motives.

The monotonous life that Josephine was
now leading, the constant restraint, the necessity for reserve, the tediousness of listening to
the weak talk of the old lady, and the repug-
nance she felt for the society of her fellow-
servants, were almost more than Josephine
could bear, and only her strong resolution to
go through with what she had undertaken kept
her at Bewdley. As she began to see how
completely Miss Otterbourne was deceived in
her servants, how she was cheated, and what a
demoralising influence in the place the trusty
butler was, she became uneasy in mind. She
did not like to allow her mistress to continue
in her delusion, and yet she was averse from
telling tales of her fellow-domestics.

The liking which Miss Otterbourne showed
for her excited the jealousy of the female
servants and the suspicion of Mr. Vickary.

This latter saw that he would not be able to influence Josephine and get her under his power. He was irritated at the contempt she showed him, and aware that she saw through and mistrusted him. He also saw that she was acquiring a preponderating influence over the mistress, which threatened his supremacy.

Josephine had more to think about than her own past troubles; but, unfortunately, those concerns which now occupied her thoughts were in themselves troubles. She missed her old freedom. She was shy of asking a favour of Miss Otterbourne, or she would have entreated to be given a bedroom to herself. The old lady did not know that she had not one. The domestic arrangements were left to the housekeeper, and those maids were given separate rooms who stood highest in her favour. At night Josephine hardly enjoyed refreshing sleep; she was not so much tired out with her work as fagged—her nerves were overwrought, not her muscles. What would she not now have given for a row on the sea or a stroll by herself in the garden. Sometimes the oppressiveness of her life threatened to drive her mad, and she made efforts to think of the sea, the gulls, the passing ships, to give breath and space to her mind, that was becoming cramped in Bewdley life.

While she read in the evenings to Miss Otterbourne her mind was absent, for the books which the old lady selected were uninteresting to Josephine. She, like Aunt Judith, was a veal-eater, and must have her mental diet devoid of the blood of ideas and the firmness of intellectual growth. Josephine had been so independent hitherto that the constraint of having in all things to submit to the will of another, to hear ineptitudes without replying, to go through a mechanical round of duties that led to nothing, were an especial trial to her. But she had the clear sense to see that it was a schooling she needed. She was learning self-restraint.

One evening the old lady was tired of the reading, did not care for patience, and as she had a little of the fretfulness induced by nettle-rash still about her, she began to grumble at never being able to hear a bit of music. With diffidence, and yet eagerness, Josephine volunteered to play and sing. She was diffident because she did not know how her mistress would take the offer; she was eager because she had not touched the piano since she left Hanford, and her soul was one that hungered and thirsted for music—a soul that could only find its full expression in pain or pleasure through music. Thus it came about that

Richard Cable heard her sing on the night he was lingering under the trees of the park.

The little old lady was not without that atmosphere of romance hanging about her heart that enlarged and transformed common objects and gave them ephemeral and fantastic values and shapes. She thought about what Mrs. Sellwood had told her of Josephine, and as she had taken a great fancy for Josephine she wanted to learn more. She wrote for particulars to her sister, but unsuccessfully, and every attempt to wrest her story from the girl equally failed. As she had so few facts on which to build, she fell back on conjecture, and speedily came to treat her conjectures as assured realities. There could be no question that Josephine was a lady, the child of gentlefolks, who had been suddenly ruined—so she supposed —by the failure of the great Coast of Guinea Bank, which had recently brought down so many families. She was an orphan, and had lost everything, and she had fled her old home and its associations owing to a love affair with a gentleman of position to whom she had been engaged, but who, having no resources himself, had broken off the match on her losing her fortune. Miss Otterbourne had in former days had several offers; but as she never could assure herself that the suitors were not in love with her estate rather than herself, she had refused them all; and now, in her old age, had a longing for a little romance, and a desire to take some part in the great concert of love that bursts from all creation, if she were only to play a little feeble accompaniment to the song of another. What a flutter it produces in an old heart on which hopes and loves have flashed and flickered and died out to white dust, to be able, before the last death-chill falls, to assist at the kindling, or to fan when lighted, or to sit by and hearken to the roar of a love-fire! So poor old Miss Otterbourne, having made out to her own satisfaction and sincere conviction that Josephine was in love and had been badly treated, turned the matter about in her mind, and schemed whether it were possible for her to take up the broken engagement and hammer and weld it together again. How she was to do this she did not know. She did not even know the gentleman. But again imagination went to work, and showed her that he was endeavouring to get into a Government situation. Miss Otterbourne knew and was connected with persons of position and influence, and might possibly induce them to get him a secretaryship or a colonial appointment. The kind little heart made its plans. The letters were thought out, and the list of those to whom application was to be made was drawn up. All that Miss Otterbourne needed to know to put all her engines in play was the name and position of the man. But when she approached the subject, however delicately, Josephine winced, changed colour, trembled, and entreated permission to leave the room.

'There is no help for it,' said Miss Otterbourne to herself; 'I must wait till I have gained her confidence. Poor young people! poor dear girl! She is growing thin and pale here. I can see the change in her. Hope deferred maketh the heart sick. It is only hope deferred, not extinguished. I am clever in these matters; I will make all right in time.'

Miss Otterbourne was warmly attached to her nephew, Captain Sellwood, who would succeed to Bewdley after her decease, when he would assume by royal license the name and arms of Otterbourne in addition to Sellwood. The old lady had much family pride in her, and loved to talk of the family greatness, its achievements and its matches in the past. It was a sad thing that Cholmondely Otterbourne, her brother, had died early, and that thus the direct male representation ceased. As the old lady loved to talk, and loved especially to talk of her nephew, on whom her ambition concentrated, she was not silent with Josephine.

'I suppose you have seen him, Cable?' she said. 'If you know Mrs. Sellwood, you have no doubt seen the captain. He is a very fine man, and has such splendid eyes, like those of an ox. I wish he would marry. I am getting to be an old woman and I want to see the young generation settled and another rising about it. I should be happy, I think, quite happy, with little grand-nephews and nieces, nephews especially, trotting about these passages and up and down the stairs. I am afraid that Captain Sellwood must have met with disappointment. You have not heard of such a rumour, have you, Cable?'

'There has been no such tale, Miss Otterbourne, as far as I am aware.'

'I cannot conceive of a girl refusing him; he is so handsome, so dignified, and has such eyes, such ox-like eyes! If he has been refused, it must have been by some great heiress, who thinks overweeningly of herself, or by a duke's daughter, or a baroness in her own right. You have seen Captain Sellwood, I suppose, Cable?'

'Yes, ma'am, I have seen him.' She always spoke respectfully to Miss Otterbourne, as a servant to a mistress.

'What do you think of him? Have you ever seen his equal?—Except——' The old lady laughed. 'That is not quite a fair question.' She assumed a roguish air. 'Every girl thinks one man the ideal of what man should be, but after—after that one, eh, Cable?'

Josephine hesitated; then evaded the answer by saying : 'I spoke the exact truth, Miss Otterbourne, about there being no reports circulating concerning Captain Sellwood; but I believe it is true, and Mr. and Mrs. Sellwood know it, that he was refused.'

'Who was she?' asked Miss Otterbourne.

'A very unworthy person,' answered Josephine.

That the captain was certain to visit Bewdley, and that she would have to meet him—she in the capacity of a servant—occurred to Josephine, and made her uneasy. But on further consideration this uneasiness passed away; it was bred of pride, and her pride was much broken. The prospect that he would come to Bewdley gave her courage and hope. Before he arrived he would have been prepared to see her; his father or mother would be certain to do that.

She thought a good deal about him, as Miss Otterbourne spoke of him so frequently, and she trusted that his arrival would relieve her from one of her great distresses. She could mention to him the condition of affairs in the house. As heir to the estate, as the person responsible next to her mistress, he ought to be told everything. Then he could act as he saw fit. She would have fulfilled her duty, and the responsibility would rest on the proper shoulders.

'Captain Sellwood comes on Tuesday,' said Miss Otterbourne one day. 'Tell Mrs. Grundy to have the Blue Room ready.'

Josephine drew a long breath. 'I am so glad!' she said. The exclamation escaped her unintentionally. Miss Otterbourne looked surprised, and then annoyed, and said no more to her that evening.

# CHAPTER XLVI.

### A CHUM.

Once, annually, whilst he was in England, did Captain Sellwood pay his aunt a visit. He stayed with her a fortnight; and she took him round to show him to her old friends, and show him the young ladies of the neighbourhood among whom he was at liberty to pick and choose—ladies by birth and breeding, and with at least something to bring with them. As yet he had not picked and chosen in the region round Bewdley; he had contented himself with exciting the admiration of the old ladies, to whom he devoted himself with more eagerness than to the young. They were his aunt's cronies, and he made an effort to please his aunt by showing courtesy to her friends.

The family coach went to the station to meet the captain, and Miss Otterbourne awaited his arrival impatiently. Josephine's heart was in a flutter. 'Shall I leave the room?' she asked, suddenly rising from her needlework in

the window. Miss Otterbourne had got into
the way of making her sit in the same room
with her much of her time.

'No, Cable,' answered the old lady—'no
need for that. You have, I daresay, seen the
captain, and he will probably know you.'

In fact, Miss Otterbourne was curious to
observe how they met; for she knew nothing
for certain about Josephine's origin, nor of the
extent of her acquaintance, nor of its character,
with the Sellwoods.

Josephine remained, but stood silent, in the
window, withdrawn as much as possible from
sight. Captain Sellwood came in, and was
greeted with love and pride by his aunt. 'My
dear fellow! How you have grown! But—I
do believe I see a careworn expression in your
face, as if the course of something—something
—had not run smooth.'

He turned abruptly from her and came
directly to Josephine, who, in spite of her
efforts to remain composed, coloured and trembled. 'We have met before—at Hanford,' he
said, with a bow and extended hand; but
whether he spoke to explain his conduct to his
aunt, or to introduce himself to Josephine, who
might not recollect him, Miss Otterbourne could
not discover.

'You will be pleased to hear that the rector

and my mother are in flourishing condition,' he went on. 'I hope I may be able to inform them, when I write, that you are well and happy.' He spoke civilly, formally, yet kindly; and what he said might have been addressed indiscriminately to a lady or a lady's-maid.

'The rogue!' said Miss Otterbourne to herself. 'He, also, wants to keep me in the dark. There is some mystery; but I shall worm it out.'

Josephine kept away from the drawing-room whilst the captain was there; her mistress did not need her when she had her nephew to talk to. She hoped to have an opportunity of speaking with him in private before long, that she might relieve her mind, after which it was her intention to leave the service of Miss Otterbourne. It did not advantage her to remain there longer. Her mistress had drawn her into association with herself, and she could associate with ladies as at Hanford. As for the servants at Bewdley, she did not wish to be on terms of familiarity with them. They did not represent the class to which Richard belonged. She must seek representatives of his order elsewhere.

One evening, the housemaid who shared her room told her that a sister and cousin had come to Bewdley and had asked her to meet them and walk with them to the station. She had, however, her duties in the house, and could not go out, leaving these neglected. As for the under-housemaid, she was engaged with her own work, and could not be trusted to arrange the rooms—would Josephine mind relieving her of this for an hour or two. ' It's the captain's two rooms have to be looked after,' said the young woman. ' If you'll do this for me to-day, Cable, I'll help you what I can another time.'

Josephine at once, good-naturedly, consented.

Captain Sellwood occupied the best bedroom, with a small sitting-room adjoining, and on the other side a dressing-room. He did not care for a fire in his bedroom ; but there was one in the sitting-room, and there his aunt allowed him to smoke. He had no valet with him to attend to his clothes ; and after he was dressed for dinner, the housemaid folded those he had taken off and put them away, and got the room ready for the night. The sitting-room had to be made tidy : the scraps of letters and envelopes to be picked up ; his newspaper to be folded and placed on the table ; his cigar end, left on the mantelshelf, to be buried in the red depths of the fire ; a flower-glass upset on the side-table, to be refilled, the blossoms rearranged, and the water to be wiped up. How untidy men are ! — No, not all men — not Richard. And had not Josephine been just as careless when in her own house?

She put everything together in the sitting-room. Captain Sellwood had worn gloves lined with swansdown, which his mother had insisted on his wearing whilst on the journey ; but either the moth had got into them, or the down was badly put on at first, and, as he found the wool coming off, whilst he was smoking he amused himself with picking it off the inside of his gloves and throwing little tufts on the floor, where it adhered to the pile of the Brussels carpet. The collecting of this down engaged Josephine some time, and she said to herself : 'If people only knew the trouble they give by their want of consideration !' and then remembered she would have done the same in former years. She was engaged picking the particles out of the carpet pile, when the bed-room door opened and Captain Sellwood came in, with one patent leather boot on his foot and the other in his hand. Josephine looked up as the door opened, and rose.

'Oh,' said he, 'I am sorry. There is a peg in the sole that hurts me, and I have come for the poker to drive it down.'

Josephine rose from her knees, colouring.

'Do not let me disturb you,' he said. 'I will go away.' He had a crimson silk stocking on his unshod foot.

'Shall I knock down the peg for you, Captain Sellwood?' asked Josephine. 'There is a hammer in the housemaid's cupboard.'

'Not on any consideration; but if you will kindly fetch me the hammer, I shall be grateful. I do not know the whereabouts of the said cupboard.' He held out his hand to help her up.

'What have you been about?' he asked.

'Collecting all these particles of swansdown. They are difficult to get out of the carpet.'

'I threw them there,' he said; 'but I am glad it has given me the opportunity of speaking to you alone, which I have desired, and failed to get.'

'I also,' said Josephine, 'wish to have a little private talk with you; but——' She looked round, and seeing that some one was in the corridor, and that the door of the sitting-room was open, she added: 'I will get the hammer for your boot at once.' Then she went out at the door and closed it behind her. She had a candle in her hand, and saw standing before her the butler, with a mocking expression on his sinister face.

'What are you doing there, Cable? You have no business in these rooms.'

She would rather not have answered him, and have passed on without a reply; but she considered that she had to return, and that the butler must be got rid of, so she answered with as much indifference as she could assume, that the housemaid was going to the station with her friends, and had asked her to see to the bedrooms.

'And to chat with the captain, who slipped away from table before his usual time.'

Josephine coloured at his insolence. She had taken Captain Sellwood's boot in her hand, and whether advisable or not, she must return with it. She went her way without appearing to notice the remark made by the butler. In ten minutes she returned with the boot; she had succeeded in knocking down the peg. As she came to the captain's door she looked round to see that the coast was clear, and then tapped lightly. He opened at once, and she went in.

She was nervous and agitated. The situation was not a pleasant one; and if she had not made up her mind to speak to him, she would have given him the boot at the door and not have gone in. But three or four days of his visit to his aunt had elapsed without her obtaining the opportunity she sought, and she did not see how she could obtain the desired interview without attracting attention and arousing curiosity.

Mr. Vickary was probably satisfied with the explanation she had given. If he doubted it, he could satisfy himself in the kitchen that it was genuine. Notwithstanding her bringing-up, Josephine had much guilelessness in her. She knew Captain Sellwood well, had known him since she was a child, and was aware that he was an honourable man, who would never forget the respect due to her. He knew her story—that she was married; and that she had met with trouble. That he knew why she had gone into service, she did not suppose. He was aware that she had resigned her right to the inheritance of Gabriel Gotham—all Hanford knew that; but the reasons for her so doing were not divulged. The captain, she presumed, thought she had been forced to take service because she was left penniless. That he would not press her to tell him anything she kept to herself, she was well satisfied. He was a gentleman, if a somewhat heavy one.

She closed the door behind her, and went towards Captain Sellwood with something of her old frankness, holding his boot in her hand. 'I must have a little talk with you,' she said.

'And there is no time like the present. I hold
you arrested by one foot. You shall not have
your boot till you have listened to me.'

'I am not likely to run away from you,
Mrs. Cable, unless you draw out of your quiver
some of your old arrows; then, knowing their
sharpness, I might in self-defence take to
flight.'

'No; I have broken off all their heads. I
will never hurt any one again—at least not
with them.'

'Take a chair, Mrs. Cable.'

'I had rather stand.'

'And I insist on your being seated.'

She obeyed, taking a small armchair near
the fire. He had lighted the candles on the
mantelpiece, and stood by the fire, with his
elbow on the shelf, resting on his shod foot,
with the red-stockinged foot crossed over the
other.

'The matter about which I desire to speak
to you,' she said, going at once to her point,
'concerns Miss Otterbourne. You and your
mother ought to know how she is treated by
her servants. She is robbed on all sides. She
is surrounded by perfectly unscrupulous persons, who are in league against her. There
are valuables in this house, heirlooms; nothing
is safe from their rapacity. Dear Miss Otter-

bourne is so confiding that she leaves everything about—her keys, her cheque-book ; her
drawers are not locked, and anyone can get at
her jewellery. The plate is entrusted to Mr.
Vickary, and—some one ought to be entrusted
with the looking after of Mr. Vickary. Is
there a list of the plate ? Do you think Miss
Otterbourne herself knows what family jewels
she has ? I have ventured to entreat her to
keep her bureau locked where she has some
securities—she ought to send them to her
banker's ; but she likes to retain them in her
own hands. I am sure the butler has been to
that bureau, though I will not say he has
abstracted anything. What I fear is—were
anything to happen to your aunt—suppose a
stroke, which is not impossible or improbable
at her age, then—this house would be at the
disposal of her servants. They might take
what they liked, and who would stop them ?
An old lady ought never to be left as Miss
Otterbourne is—without a relative by her to
guard her interests.'

'Dear Mrs. Cable,' said Captain Sellwood,
' my mother cannot be here. It is also out of
the question that I should. We had hoped—
when you came——'

' Exactly, that I was to be life and body
guard to her Majesty. I do not feel disposed

to be that. I tell you the state of affairs, and
then I go. I cannot remain here. Miss
Otterbourne is very kind, and I like her; but
I cannot remain. You can see that for yourself. Having revealed the misdemeanours of
my fellow-servants, I must go as well as they.'

'I do not see that.'

'I do. I could not stay. There are other
matters behind all this that I have told you;
but you know enough.'

'What is to be done?'

'What is to be done?' repeated Josephine,
with a return to her old contemptuous manner.
You are a man, a soldier, and ask me that!'

'Precisely; because I am a man and a
soldier, I know nothing about domestic matters;
I cannot engage a new set of servants.'

'But you can induce your aunt to dismiss
these.'

'And I know very well that with a new
supply she would fare no better. She has had
relays of ladies'-maids, and has demoralised
them all—made very decent girls my mother
has sent her, dishonest and given to drink.'

'Well, I have discharged my duty. It is
for you to act on the information you have
received. This house not only demoralises the
ladies'-maids, but the entire parish. Your good
old aunt, with a mind full of religion and kind-

liness, is poisoning every man, woman, and child who comes near her. Trust is a very good thing when well applied ; but trust given to the untrustworthy aggravates the evil. Why, what will become of the servant-girls of this establishment when they marry ? They have learned here to be dainty, thriftless, and dis-honest ; to take to themselves whatever comes to hand, and to use everything without consideration what it costs. They will make their husbands and families wretched and wicked.' Josephine spoke with vehemence, because she felt strongly, and had been bottling up her indignation ever since she had begun to see into the condition of affairs in the house, without the opportunity of giving it vent.

Captain Sellwood stood looking down at his unbooted foot, meditating. His face was troubled. 'It would be conferring on us the greatest favour, it would be laying us under a life-long obligation, if you would consent to stay as companion to my aunt.'

'I cannot. The captain who applies the match to the powder-room does not blow up the crew and provide for his own safety—they all go up into the air together. I cannot do what seems mean.'

'We have no claim whatever on you ; but you are here on the spot—if——'

'No, Captain Sellwood—no! How slow you are to take a no!'

Then ensued another silence.

'I have said what I had to say, and now I must go.' She made a motion to rise. He waved his hand.

'I pray you, one moment longer. About yourself. If you insist on leaving this house, where will you go?'

'I do not know. I have not considered.'

'Excuse me, Mrs. Cable. I do not want to touch on matters that I have no right to put my finger on, but—we are old acquaintances of many, many years' standing. I cannot bear to think of your being in positions to which you were not born. Do not be offended. I am a clumsy man with my tongue, as you know very well.' He spoke with such truth and kindness, such real feeling in his voice, that Josephine's heart grew soft. 'I ask no questions; I want to know nothing about any of these matters that have occurred and that have affected you; but I do pray you—I pray you—do nothing without consulting my mother; and do not—do not be too proud to take her helping hand. Indeed, you can do my mother no greater favour than ask her to help you in any and every way.'

Josephine did not answer at once. It was

not possible for her to answer with frankness without entering into an explanation of her circumstances, which she could not do to him. After thinking, and turning his boot about in her hand, she said: 'I am very sensible, Captain Sellwood, of your kindness; and I know how good and generous your dear mother is, and how I can rely as well on your father. He approves of all I have done. You must not think me wanting in generosity if I change the subject. You have drawn the conversation away from your aunt to me, and I had rather not have it turn about myself, but revert to what we spoke of at first.'

'As you will, Mrs. Cable.'

'I think that you must get a gentlewoman to live here as companion to Miss Otterbourne, and strike at once at Mr. Vickary. The housekeeper and the maid-servants are not badhearted; but no one in the household has the moral courage to withstand him. Try to induce your aunt to part with him and take a suitable companion. Then the servants' hall can be weeded leisurely.'

A tap at the door. The captain called out to come in, and Josephine looked round to see who asked admission. She was thinking only of what she was saying, and had forgotten where she was, and how strange it would

seem to any one opening the door for her to
be seated by Captain Sellwood's fire in his
private sitting and smoking room talking confidentially with him.

In the doorway stood Miss Otterbourne;
and Josephine caught a glimpse of the butler
gliding away from behind her. 'Really!' exclaimed the old lady—'really—I am surprised
—I—I——'

'There is your boot, Captain Sellwood,'
said Josephine, starting up, suddenly conscious
of her situation, and hurriedly left the room.

He took the boot, and slowly and clumsily
drew it on. He also saw what an awkward
position they had been in.

'Can you allow me a *tête-à-tête*?' asked the
old lady, somewhat stiffly; 'or—do you prefer
younger society?'

'It was,' he stammered—'my—my boot
that we were engaged upon. We are old
chums; we were chumming, aunt, only chumming.'

# CHAPTER XLVII.

## DISMISSAL.

AFTER Mr. Vickary had seen Josephine leave Captain Sellwood's room with his boot, he waited about, keeping himself concealed, till she returned with the boot and shut the door, whereupon he went to Miss Otterbourne in the drawing-room, whither she had retired after dinner, and was waiting for her nephew to rejoin her, when he had sat sufficiently long over the wine and dessert.

'I beg your pardon, ma'am,' said the butler; 'I do hope I'm not taking a liberty, ma'am; but may I ask if you told Cable to go in and out as she liked of the captain's apartments?'

'Of course not, Vickary.'

'I'm sorry to trouble you, ma'am. I see her running in there a score of times—it's remarked by the servants, and rather unpleasant, and Mrs. Grundy says she has given no such orders; so we thought it best, ma'am, if I were to ask if you, ma'am, had empowered her so to do. You will excuse me, ma'am, but when there is talk—and when the young woman tells lies about it——'

'Lies, Vickary?'

'Well, ma'am, just now I see her go in there, and the captain there too. I said to her that I didn't consider it quite right—it was not her place; and she told me that the house-keeper had set her to attend to the room, which, ma'am, I knew not to be true.'

'The captain is in the dining-room.'

'I'm sorry to differ from you, ma'am; but he went up very quickly to his rooms, and Cable was in after him directly. It must be very unpleasant, ma'am, for a young gentleman to be so run after, and it makes talk in the house.'

Miss Otterbourne was much astonished and greatly indignant. 'Do you mean to tell me, Vickary, that she is there now?'

'I believe so, madam.'

'And the captain is there?'

'I saw him by the fire; and Cable shut the door after her when she went in.'

'Go and fetch her at once.—No. I will go myself. I really—upon my word—to say the least—how inconsiderate.'

The old lady was very angry. She raised

herself with difficulty from her armchair, drew a silk handkerchief over her shoulders, as a protection against damp or draught outside the room, and walked in the direction of her nephew's suite of apartments. When she opened the door and saw Josephine seated in an armchair on one side of the fire and the captain standing near her, in earnest conversation, she was as irritated as if her nettlerash had suddenly come out over her temper.

As soon as Josephine had left the room, Miss Otterbourne said—she was panting from having ascended a flight, and walked fast—'I—I am surprised. These may be Indian barrack habits, but—but——'

Captain Sellwood managed to get his boot on; his face was nearly the colour of his stocking.

'And only partly dressed too,' gasped Miss Otterbourne, 'half shod, and—and, with a hole in your stocking sole. Good heavens, how indelicate!'

'There was a peg in the boot,' explained Captain Sellwood.

'My dear Algernon, there generally are pegs in boots.'

'I mean—it hurt me, and I asked Josephine——'

'Josephine!'

'My dear aunt, we have known each other since children.'

'Oh!' The nettlerash was alleviated. But presently it came out again. 'That does not explain her coming to visit you in your private room, sitting in your armchair.'

'Where would you have had her sit, aunt?'

'Algernon—she is a servant.'

'Aunt—she is a lady.'

'A real lady would never have run after you into your private apartments.'

'She did not run after me. She did not know I was there. She was picking up the swansdown I had inconsiderately strewed on the carpet, when I came in.'

'Then she should considerately have gone out.'

'I asked her for a hammer.'

'She had no right here.—And are you aware, Algernon, that you have had a hole the size of a threepenny piece in the sole of your foot, at the—heel, exposed? If you had had any sense of decency, you would have kept your foot flat on the carpet, instead of turning it up.—I don't care whether she is a lady by birth and breeding; she is no lady at heart, or she would never have sat here half an hour or three-quarters, staring at a bit of your heel exposed, the size of a threepenny piece. That alone stamps her. She has a nasty mind, and must go.'

'My dear aunt—surely you are hard in judging. There was a peg in my boot that stood up, and that hurt my foot, and no doubt at the same time worked the hole in my stocking.'

'That is very probable,' said Miss Otterbourne. 'But I should like to know, were you aware it was there?'

'No; I felt my heel painful; I do not think I noticed that my stocking was rent.'

'That excuses you, but not her.'

'Perhaps she did not see it.'

'Nonsense; of course she saw it.'

'Aunt, do sit down——'

'In that armchair vacated by her!—No! She has been looking at the hole in your stocking from that armchair.—I couldn't do it.'

'Do what, aunt?'

'Sit in the chair after that'—the old lady was now very angry, and very convinced that Josephine was no lady—'gloating on it—positively gloating on it.'

'If any blame attaches to any one, it is to me,' said Captain Sellwood. 'I came in here out of my bedroom, with my boot in my hand, for the poker, with which——'

'Why did you not ring for John Thomas?'

'It was not worth while. When I came in, I found her on her knees picking up the bits of down, and I asked her for a hammer, or she offered one, I do not recollect which ; and then she whipped the boot out of my hand and went off with it. It was most good-natured of her.'

'I object to young women being good-natured with young men. Good-nature may go too far.'

'And then I asked her to sit down. I wanted to talk to her about Hanford, and my mother, and mutual acquaintances. I was awfully sorry for her, to see her in such circumstances.'

'I disapprove of young men being, as you call it, " awfully sorry " for distressed damsels ; there is no knowing to what this awful sorry may lead.'

'My dear aunt, it was natural. I have known her, and she was my playmate since we were children. I do like her ; I always have liked her. Why, if I were in reduced circumstances, you, aunt, would not cut me.'

'No '—slightly mollified. ' But I am your aunt, and not a young creature. That makes mountains of difference.—And pray, is it only her reduced circumstances that stirs up in you such awful sorrow ? She has had some other trouble, I know. Are you acquainted with her intended? Have you brought her a message from him?'

'She has no intended.'

'Then it is broken off! I was sure she has had an affair of the heart, she has looked so peaky and pale since she has been here.'

'I do not know anything about her heart affairs,' said Captain Sellwood. 'I know that one or two fellows have been awfully fond of her.'

'Indeed! Is it possible that one who has confessed to awful sorrow should also allow awful fondness? That it leads to awful chumming, I have seen with my eyes.'

Captain Sellwood did not answer. He had spoken inconsiderately, and his aunt had taken advantage of his mistake.

'Good gracious, Algernon! You don't mean to tell me that there has been an attachment in this quarter?'

'No attachment,' he said, looking down and knitting his brows. 'For an attachment, the chain must hold at both ends.'

'Merciful powers, Algernon! Can your mother have sent this chum of yours here to be out of your way!—You were so infatuated, there was no knowing what lengths you would go, and my dear sister hoped that by putting a distance between you——'

'No, aunt—nothing of the sort.'

'But I must get to the bottom of this. There is something kept from me. Is it true that you have—that you have—harboured an unfortunate passion for this young person—this chum, as you call her?'

'I did love the young lady. We have known each other since we were children—at least since she was a little girl and I a big boy. She was so lively, so daring, so witty, I could not help loving her. But that is over now.'

'I should hope so—I should hope so indeed. A servant-maid—a servant-maid in my house! Lord have mercy on us! It is a wonder to me you did not turn Mohammedan in India, and put your neck under Juggernaut's car.'

'My dear aunt, what have Juggernaut and his car, and Mohammedanism and Josephine, to do with each other?'

'What a world we live in!' groaned Miss Otterbourne. 'Radicalism everywhere!'

'You forget, aunt, that she belonged to the class of life to which I belong. I may tell you this—that she has inherited a very handsome estate, but has conscientious scruples, which I do not understand, because I do not know the circumstances, against her enjoying it; and rather than violate her conscience, she has

come into service to you. I honour and respect her for it, aunt!'

'But—she *is* a servant. She is my lady's-
maid. It does not matter one hair whether she
be heiress to untold millions or be a household
drudge, the moral indelicacy is the same. She
ought never to have sat here in your chair,
talking to you when you had a hole in your
stocking.—No, Algernon, you may say what
you will—you may try to throw dust in my
old eyes, but I shall never get over that hole
in your stocking.' She had said enough and
heard enough, and she left the room.—' Smoke
your cigar,' she said as she left, ' and then
come down to me. I presume you can light it
without the assistance of your *chum*.'

When the old lady reached her drawing-
room, she was so hot that she sank into her
chair and fanned herself for several minutes
without getting any cooler. She rang the bell,
and bade John Thomas send her Cable at
once; and in two minutes Josephine came to
her.

'Cable,' said Miss Otterbourne, fanning
herself vigorously, 'I am surprised and offended. I *did* suppose you knew your place
better, and had more delicacy than to sit in a
room with a gentleman who had a hole in his
stocking.'

G 2

'Had he?  I did not know it, ma'am.'

'Did not know it?  Of course you knew it!  I saw by the direction of your eyes, the instant I came in, that you were examining it.'

'I did not give it a thought, even if I saw it, and I do not believe I did that.  But, surely, ma'am, there is no harm in that.'

'No harm in sitting in an armchair in the same room with a gentleman, a captain in Her Majesty's service, who has been in India, when he is in a condition of partial undress!  In such a house as this, such transgressions cannot be passed over.  My nephew informs me that you have been old acquaintances; but old acquaintanceship does not remove all the barriers of female delicacy, and give a woman liberty to look at a man's foot without his boot covering it.  It is perhaps allowed us to know that the other sex has feet, because they are mentioned in the Bible; but we know it as we know that we have antipodes, by faith, not by sight.'  She fanned herself with a vehemence which made her hot, and fluttered the little silver barrels on both sides of her brow.  'Cable—it does not please me to have simultaneously under my roof a nephew as a visitor and an old acquaintance of his—*chum* he called you—as a lady's-maid.  The situation is incon-

gruous, and leads, as I have seen to-night, to
injudicious conduct, which may, which has
occasioned scandal ; and such a house as this
must be maintained in its dignity and irre-
proachability.  Either the captain, my nephew,
or you, my servant, must leave, and leave
without delay.'

'Of course, Miss Otterbourne, I will go.'

'If you can make it convenient to depart
to-morrow, you will oblige.  I am sorry to say
this, but—it is quite impossible for me to have
my nephew and you under the same roof
together.  I have the greatest reliance on his
discretion ; I wish I could say the same of
yours.  You shall receive, as is your due, a
month's wage, because you leave to suit my
convenience.  There is an excellent Refuge
for domestics and governesses out of place at
Bath, to which I subscribe, and you can go
there till you hear of a situation.'

'Thank you, Miss Otterbourne, but I shall
not stay in Bath.'

'Will you go back to Hanford ? '

Josephine shook her head.

'I am sorry—I am sincerely sorry.  There
is so much good about you, so much that I have
liked ; but, under the circumstances, I cannot
retain you.  It would not be right ; and in this
house—from myself down, I believe, to the

scullery-maid and the boy who cleans the knives—I trust we all try to do that which is right. Mr. Vickary is a burning and a shining light, and Mrs. Grundy, hardly less so—a moon beside the sun. But I will not speak of this. I never dismiss a servant except for some gross offence—and I really do not believe such has occurred—without some little testimonial of my regard; so you must allow me to present you with a five-pound note in addition to your wage. You have been guilty of an indiscretion —I firmly trust, unpremeditated.'

'O Miss Otterbourne!'

'Where do you purpose going?' asked the old lady. 'I cannot possibly permit you to depart without some knowledge that you are going to a place where you will be cared for.'

'I am going'—Josephine looked down, then up—'yes, I am going down into Cornwall.'

'Into Cornwall! Where to?'

'To my husband.'

'Cable—what? Husband! I do not understand.'

'To my husband, madam.'

'You are a married woman?'

Josephine bowed.

'Goodness gracious me!—But that somewhat alters the complexion of affairs. A married woman ! Does my nephew know that ? '

Josephine bowed again.

' A married woman !—But where is your wedding-ring ? '

' In my bosom.'

Miss Otterbourne fanned herself fastly, not with wrath, but with the agitation occasioned by amazement. ' Merciful powers ! — you married ! Who would have thought it ! And so young, and so pretty ! It hardly seems possible. But—if you are married—it is not so dreadfully improper that you should know men have feet under their boots. I do not say it is right ; but it is not so very wrong that—that you should have seen a hole in my nephew's stocking, because married women do know that such things occur.'

Josephine smiled ; she thought Miss Otterbourne was about to retract her discharge, so she said : ' Madam, I cannot stay here. I have explained my reasons to Captain Sellwood, who will tell you after I am gone. Now I have made my resolve, I go direct to my husband.'

The door of the drawing-room opened and the butler came in. He advanced deferentially towards Miss Otterbourne, and stood awaiting her permission to speak.

'What is it, Vickary? Do you want anything?'

'It is Cable, madam.'

'Well—what of Cable, Vickary?'

'Please, madam, Cable's husband have come
to fetch her away.'

# CHAPTER XLVIII.

## A REPETITION.

ONE Sunday when Richard Cable was at home after he and his children and mother had dined, he said : 'Now, my dears, we will all go out and walk together, and see the place where my new house shall stand with seven red windows.'

Then the little maids had their straw hats, trimmed with blue ribbons, put on, and their pinafores taken off, and they marched forth with their father on the road towards Rosscarrock. It was winter, but mild and warm ; and the sun shone ; red beech and oak leaves lay thick in the furrows and sides of the road, and under the ash-trees the way was strewn as with scraps of black string. The leaves had rotted, leaving the mid-ribs bare. The starlings were about in droves, holding parliament, or church, or gossiping parties. The holly, grown to trees in the hedges and woods, was covered in the hedges with scarlet berries ; but bare of fruit in the wood, where the shadow of the oaks and beech had interfered with the setting of the flower.

When Cable came to the coveted spot, whom should he see but Farmer Tregurtha! In fact, from his house, Tregurtha had heard the chattering of the little voices in the clear air, just like the chattering of the starlings, and some one had said to him : ' Uncle Dick be coming along wi' all his maidens.' Then Tregurtha had walked across the fields to meet him.

Among the Cornish, any old man, or man past the middle age, is entitled Uncle. Now, Richard had not attained the middle point of life ; but the St. Kerian folk did not know his age, and thought him older than he really was, partly because he had so large a family, but chiefly because his trouble and his gloomy temper had given a look of age beyond his years.

Things had not gone well with Tregurtha. He had been engaged in a long lawsuit with Farmer Hamlyn about a right of way, and had lost, it was whispered, several hundreds of pounds, because he was so obstinate that he carried his case by appeal from court to court. Cable knew this very well, and would not have been the Cable he had become if unready to profit by it.

'Hulloh, uncle!' called Tregurtha. 'Glad to see you home again, and in the midst of your stars, as the sun among the seven planets. —Ah! folks always say that children bring luck, and a seventh maid is born with hands that scatter gold. Luck has hopped off my shoulders and lighted on yours.—Have you still a fancy for Summerleaze?'

'Where law is handled, luck leaks out,' answered Richard Cable. 'Come into the road, and we'll have a word together.' Then he bade the seven little girls hold hands and walk on beyond earshot.

They were some time together; but before they parted, Cable had agreed to purchase Summerleaze and to give for it a hundred and fifty pounds. Tregurtha was glad to get that price for it. Thus it was that the land became Cable's, and the first step was taken towards the fulfilment of his dream and the realisation of his ambitious scheme. But he was not yet prepared to build; for that he needed more money.

Once again he was at Bewdley, and he went there with the determination of seeing Josephine, without allowing her to see him, but when he was there, some indistinct feeling held him back, and he went away without having caught sight of her; but he had made inquiries concerning her of his landlady, Mrs. Stokes, without appearing to interest himself especially about her. No sooner was he away, with his face turned homewards, than he regretted his lack of courage, and made a fresh resolve to see her.

And now that he was possessed of land, he became more eager after money and more adventurous in his speculations. He was never at rest. He denied himself the supreme pleasure life had for him—the pleasure of being at home with his children. He travelled over the north of Cornwall, from Bodmin and Camelford to Stratton, and through the poor land from the Tamar to Holsworthy and Hatherleigh, buying stock and sending it off. He purchased all the calves he could in the dairy country and sold them to the stock-rearing farmers, and the money was never idle in his pocket; he turned it and turned it, and it multiplied in his hands.

Then Cable went to Mr. Spry, the mason, and ordered him to build the house. 'I will have it a long house,' he said. 'The ground rises so sharp behind, that it cannot be more than one room deep, and so I will have seven red windows upstairs—three on one side and three on the other, and two below to right and two to left and two shams, and over the door

in the middle a window. That will make seven
windows in the front upstairs and four below;
and on one side of the door shall be the dwell-
ing part for me and my children; and on the
other side of the door shall be the kitchen and
back-kitchen; and there shall be a great sort
of lobby and hall in the middle, where the
children can romp of a rainy day; and because
the land falls away so rapidly in front, there
must be a flight of stone steps up to the main
entrance.'

When this was settled, away went Richard
Cable again, and now he went to Bewdley, and
as he travelled he thought: 'I should like *her*
to see my land and my house that I am building,
and how I am going to make myself a gentleman
and all my maidens to be ladies, with no help
from her, all out of my own work with my head
and hands.'

In this frame of mind he arrived at Bewdley,
but without having come to a decision whether
he would see her or not. Perhaps, some day,
when Red Windows was finished, he would
have a large photograph taken of it, with the
colours put in, green for the trees, and red for
the windows, and send it to her by post. When
she saw the picture and read under it, 'Red
Windows, the property of Mr. Richard Cable,'
then she would learn how great and rich a man

he had become, and how he throve when separated from her.

He was at the Bewdley tavern again, and he looked at Mary Stokes, and told her mother that the girl was growing into a fine little woman. 'Down in the west where I am,' said he, 'there are no girls, only maidens. If you speak of a girl, they either don't know what you mean, or think you mean something insulting. I suppose, now, in a little while you'll be thinking of getting Mary a situation in the great house? What will she take to?—housemaids' work or the kitchen? The nursery is out of the question where a baby's voice has not been heard for over half a century.'

Mrs. Stokes shook her head. 'No, Mr. Cable, my little girl don't go there.'

'But why not? You're a tenant under the lady.'

'I shouldn't wish it,' said Mrs. Stokes, mysteriously. 'I don't mind saying as much to you, as you're a stranger, and can't or wouldn't hurt me with Mr. Vickary or the old lady—but, I can't afford to send my Mary there.'

'Can't afford! Is it like an appointment in the army, more cost than gain?'

Mrs. Stokes again shook her head. 'You see, Mr. Cable, things in that house ain't as they ought to be; and I wouldn't have my child there not for a score of pounds. The old lady, she's good and innocent, and thinks she'll make all the world about her into Christians; but, Lord love you! that house is not a Christian household outside of her sitting-room.'

'What do you mean?' asked Richard, uneasily working on his chair.

'I don't mind saying it before you, because you're a stranger, and wouldn't hurt a fly, let alone me; but Mr. Vickary is a bad lot, and he leads the old madam by the nose. Bless you! if it was only picking and stealing, I'd shut my mouth and say nothing, for what is riches given to some for, but that those who haven't may help themselves out of their abundance? But'—she began to scrub the table—'there be things go on there, or is said to go on, that would make decent mothers shy of sending their servants into that house.'

Richard's face became red as blood, and his hair bristled on his head. If Mrs. Stokes had looked at him instead of looking at the table she was scouring, she would have been startled by his face.

'Lord, Mr. Cable, when you come to think of it, it is wonderful what a lot of evil is done in the world by them as intend to do good—I do in truth believe, more than by the out-and-out wicked ones. And I take it the reason is, your well-intending people begin their bettering of others by taking leave of common sense themselves.—There comes Mr. Polkinghorn; don't say nothing of all this to him.'

'How do you do, Mr. Cable? How are we, Mrs. Stokes?' asked the pleasant footman entering, rubbing his hands. 'A little frosty to-night. I shall be glad of brandy-and-water hot, please, and sugar.—How go the calves in the van, sir, and the kids at home?'

'And how is my namesake, Mr. Polkinghorn?'

'Oh, the lovely Cable!' He shrugged his shoulders. 'I don't think she'll be much longer with us.'

'What—dying?' The colour deserted Richard's brow.

'O dear, no! Very far from that—a little too much alive—that is all.'

'I do not take your meaning, Mr. Polkinghorn.'

'I have a tendency to cloudiness,' answered the flunky. 'I have generally been thought a wag.—Thank you, Mrs. Stokes. This is real cognac, I hope, and the water boiling?' Having been satisfied on this score, Mr. Polkinghorn poured himself out a stiff glass. 'The cold settles in the stomach, Mr. Cable,' he explained.

'What about my namesake?' again asked
Richard, whose face was serious, and who sat
with his hand to his head, looking across the
table at the footman.

'Oh, as to Miss C.—we'll use initials, and
that obviates the chance of giving offence—
she's a high-flyer.'

'She is proud and disdainful, you mean?'

'That she is. But that is not what I allude
to.' He took a pipe and filled it with tobacco.
'You see, my dear sir, we've had our captain
staying with us.'

'Who is your captain?'

'The old woman's nephew, Captain Sellwood.'

Cable's fingers twitched; the nails went into
his brow.

'I don't myself give credence to all I hear;
but there's a talk that the lovely C. is setting
her cap at the captain. That's a pun, you will
understand.'

Cable did not laugh.

The flunky explained: 'I am a joker.—I
don't pretend to say where fact ends and
fiction begins,' Mr. Polkinghorn went on to say,
'because what I have heard has come from the
lips of old V., and old Mr. V. can colour
matters to suit himself, just as a blancmange
can be made pink with a drop of cochineal;

or, if you prefer another similitude, he can flavour his facts to his taste, as you can any pudding with ratafia or vanilla. There must be something to go upon, or you can't colour or flavour at all. That stands to reason.—Are you particularly interested in Miss Cable?'

'She bears my name,' said Richard sternly.

'Ah, quite so! I understand the feeling. I myself could not endure the thought of a Polkinghorn doing a dirty act; but—I don't believe a Polkinghorn could so demean himself —the name would hold him up.'

'What is the fact, coloured or clear?'

'Oh, I can't say. V. will have it that Miss C. has been carrying it on with the captain, and there has been a rumpus accordingly; and the old woman has had to interfere, and—I do not believe that she will let the beautiful and fascinating C. remain much longer with us— that is what V. says; but V. has never taken warmly to the C.; she has been short with him.'

Then Cable stood up, and without another word, went out of the inn—he went out forgetful that he had not his hat upon his head, and he walked hastily in the direction of Bewdley Manor.

How wonderful is man's life! It turns about like a wheel, and he does those things

to-day which he did some time agone. But no
—not those things exactly. They differ in
particulars, but in direction they are the same.
His life moves in spirals, ever reverting to
where it ran before, but never quite going over
the same ground. On one memorable evening
Josephine had been in Brentwood Hall, and
Richard had run to bring her thence, hatless,
coatless, breathless. Now he went, by night,
to another great house, also through a park,
hatless, breathless, but not on this occasion
coatless—there was the difference. On that
former occasion, Josephine was the most
honoured guest in the great house; now she was
the least esteemed servant in this great house.

For many thousands of years men believed
that storms blew over their heads, tearing up
trees, unroofing houses, flashing with electric
bolts, pursuing a direct course. They held
that storms never swerved to one side or the
other till they had expended their violence.
Now we are told that no storm travels thus—
they all move in a rotary course; they whirl
across the earth and sea like aerial spinning-
tops. We have supposed, and we still suppose,
that men go straight courses from birth to
death; but is it so? Is not the spirit of man
a blast of the Great Spirit that sweeps along
through life in a succession of revolutions? Do

we not find, when we look back at our own
past history, that we do again and yet again
the same things—that again and yet again we
drive in the same direction one day, and in the
opposite on the morrow? I myself, when I
shut my eyes and hold my face in my hands,
can hear the spirit within me whirling and
humming, and eager to sweep me away into
some folly that I committed a few months ago,
and vowed then I would never commit again.

We think the same thoughts, as we speak
the same words, and, alas, tell the same old
stories, and crack the same old jokes, day after
day, in our little teetotum spin. What an
amount of impetus there is in our movement!
what a whir, what a hum we make!—but what
a little movement forward in the straight line
there is for the vast amount of rotary hurry
and noise! On this evening, Richard Cable
was doing very much the same thing he had
done on another evening, the memory of which
still scorched his brain; and he was doing that
which he had resolved never to do again. He
did it with a difference. We all do our little
rounds with a difference. He went this time
with his coat on his back; but he was as hot,
and as agitated, and as breathless as before.

See what an advance the man had made!
He went in his coat; though, I grant, he went

this time in his coat chiefly because he had his
coat on his back when the impulse started him
to go. Still this was an advance, a distinct
advance.

Richard Cable stood still when he came to
the house. He tried to collect his thoughts
and resolve what to do. But the dog in the
backyard began to bark furiously, and its bark
distracted him ; he could not gather his ideas.
He knew that Josephine was in a place which
she could not remain in without some taint
adhering to her. She was under the same
roof with the man who had loved her and had
proposed to her ; a man of her own class, a
man whom she had known for long. Richard
put from him at once the thought that she
was, what the footman said, consciously
'making up to' the captain ; but he was by
no means sure that unconsciously she might be
drawn towards him.

On that other evening when he had run to
Brentwood, he had been unable to gather his
thoughts ; but he had seen clearly one thing—
that his wife ought to be with him in his great
trouble ; so now, his mind was confused, yet
one idea shone out clear through the fog of
thoughts—that his wife must not be allowed to
remain another night in Bewdley Manor. On
that other evening, he thought of himself ; on

this, he thought of her. Then, he it was who needed a stay ; now, it was not he, but she. So, with this one idea fixed in his mind, with his ears full of the noise of the dog-barking, and with the throb of the blood in the pulses in his ears, he went into the house. But how he encountered the butler, and where and how he made known what he needed, and how he was brought upstairs and confronted with Josephine and Miss Otterbourne in the great state drawing-room, that he never was able to remember distinctly. He saw everything about him through a haze, as though smoke were rising, or the carpet steamed like a ploughed field in the morning sun. He saw his wife, but she seemed to him as afar off—as if he saw her through a glass. He made no effort to collect his thoughts ; he formed no resolution as to the course he would pursue, but he said: 'I have come for my wife. Give her up to me. This is no place for her. I insist on her coming with me—at once— wherever I choose to take her.'

Then Josephine said: 'Richard—I will follow you wherever you go.'

# CHAPTER XLIX.

## A DROPPED 'S.'

RICHARD CABLE wheeling a barrow that he had borrowed from the stables, laden with Josephine's box, went out of the grounds of Bewdley Manor, and Josephine walked at his side.

'Richard,' she said, 'how comes it that you are lame?'

'You have lamed me.'

'Richard,' she said, 'how oldened you are.'

'You have oldened me.'

'And bent.'

'You have bowed my back.'

'Do not speak unkindly to me,' she pleaded. 'I know I have done wrong, and am sorry for it.'

'When you break china, can you mend it that the cracks do not show and that it will hold as before?'

She did not answer this question.

'And man's heart, when it is broken, can it

be patched up ? If you pour love into it again, does not the love run out at all sides and leave the vessel dry ? '

' You do not forgive me, Richard ? '

' I do not—I cannot.'

' Then why have you come for me now ? '

' Because you bear my name, and, to my woe, are my wife, and—I would not have you there, where a stain may come on the name, and where my wife may be—nay, is, lightly spoken of. Mind you,' continued Cable, bending between the handles of the barrow, ' I do not mistrust your conduct. Though he is there under the same roof with you who loved you, and perhaps loves you still, I have no doubt about your conduct. God spare me that! I know you to be proud and cruel, but I know also that you are not light. You have brought me down, but not to such baseness as to think that.'

' I thank you for that, Richard, at all events for that.—Where am I going now? What will you do with me ? '

' You are going now to the inn, to Mrs. Stokes. Where you go next, what I do with you after this night, I cannot tell; you shall know to-morrow. My head is like the old lightship in a chopping sea.'

As soon as they reached the tavern, Richard

brought Josephine in, and said to the landlady : 'This is my wife; take her in for the night ; give her my room. I am going out, and shall not be back before morning. If she needs anything, let her have it, and stint her not.' He said no farewell to Josephine, but went out at the door, wiping his brow on his sleeve.

He walked by the river. He had not got his stick, and he cut himself one from the hedge ; and as the night was dark and he had to grope among them for a suitable stick, he tore his hands, and they were covered with blood, and when he wiped his brow the smears came on his face. He obtained a good stout stick at last on which he could lean, and he stood resting on it by the river, looking over the slowly flowing water to the dark horizon, and the red glare in the sky beyond over Bath.

The season was autumn, the time when, at the rising of the sun, the whole face of a field and every hedge are seen to be covered with cobwebs strung with dew. And now, in the night, the air was full of these cobwebs ; one might have thought they were spun in heaven, and came down charged with water. They drifted in the light air, and the dew that rose settled on the minute fibres and weighed them down, that they came leisurely down—down through the raw night-air. They settled over

Richard's head—they fell on his face—they came on his hands, and he was forced to brush them away, because they teased him. There were other cobwebs, in his brain, confusing, teasing that, charged also with drops, bitter and salt; but these he could not sweep away—he thrust them aside, and they spread again; he squeezed them together and wrung out the brine and gall, and they unfurled and fell again over his brain. They obscured his sight of the future; they troubled his thought of the present; and they all rose, thick, teasing, even torturing out of the past; and all the myriad threads went back to one root—Josephine. But as in a web there are fibres and cross-fibres, so was it with this inner cobweb—there were some revengeful and others pitiful; some hard and others soft; some of hate and some of love; yet by night, as he stood by the water, striking now with his hand, then with his stick, at the falling cobwebs, he could not distinguish one thread from another; so one feeling was interlaced and intertangled with another, that they were not to be unravelled.

There still lurked in his mind that fear of Josephine which he had first entertained when he saw her on the stranded lightship and heard her sing the Mermaid's song; that fear which his mother had detected in him when he lay crippled at the 'Magpie,' and which she at once brought back to its true source—love. Richard Cable did not know that there remained any trace of his old love there; he thought that all his feeling for Josephine was anger and resentment; but he was not a man given to self-analysis. He was aware of the ever-presence of pain in his soul, and he knew who had hurt him, but hardly the nature of that pain. We carry about with us for many years, may be, a something in us that never allows us to forget that all is not well—a spasm of the heart, a gnawing pain in the chest, a shooting-needle in the brain, a racking cough, and we do not consult a physician: we may soon outgrow it; it came on after an overstrain, a chill, and a long rest will recover us of it. What it is we do not know; we generally attribute it to a wrong cause, and regard it as that which it is not. It is so also with our mental aches—we have them; we go on enduring them, and often wholly misinterpret them. Richard supposed that he had acted out of regard for his own name, that the fever and alarm he had felt was occasioned by no other dread; but when he sprang up from Mrs. Stokes' table and hurried to the manor-house to fetch away Josephine, he had not thought about the preservation of the name of Cable from a slur, only of her—of

her in bad moral surroundings, of her exposed
to slights, and perhaps temptations.   On this
night, the sight of her in her quiet servant's
dress, with her face pale, the eyes deep, the
lines of her countenance sharp drawn, had
strangely affected him.   He thought that it
had roused in him his full fierceness of resentment for wrong done ; but he was mistaken—
the deepest bell in the rugged belfry of his
heart had never ceased thrilling from the first
stroke dealt it ; and now it was touched again
by the sight of her face and the sound of her
voice, and the whole mass quivered with its
renewed vibrations.   Though the dew fell
heavily, Richard Cable did not feel the moisture ; and though there was frost, he was
not cold.   The night was long, but he was
unaware of its length.

He did not return to the inn till morning,
and then he had formed a plan, and he had
gained the mastery over himself.   Early though
the hour was when he arrived, he found
Josephine already down.   Contrary to his
former frank ways, he did not look her full in
the face ; he felt his weakness and would not
venture to do so.   He spoke to her only when
necessary, and with restraint in his tone.   The
voice was hard and his face drawn and cold.

'I truck my young calves to Exeter,' he

said. 'We will go thither by train. After that, you will have to come the rest of the way in my conveyance, unless you prefer the coach.'

'No,' answered Josephine; 'I will go with you.'

He drew a weary breath; he would have preferred to send her by the coach. The oppressiveness of a journey with her was not to be contemplated with composure.

'Then,' said he, 'we will start at once; that is, when I have got my calves in truck. The train is at ten-fifteen. You will be at the station. I will speak to a man to fetch your box, and I will pay him. Have it ready labelled for the Clarendon Hotel at Exeter.'

'The Clarendon! Is that where you stay when there?'

'The Clarendon is where you shall be. You will be well cared for there; it is a good hotel, the best in Exeter; it looks out on the close, and is very respectable.'

'Shall you be there, Richard?'

'No; I go elsewhere. Calves are not taken in at first-class hotels.'

'But I had rather, a thousand times rather, be with you.'

'I have my calves to suckle. I must go where I am accustomed to go, and where I can get milk for them.'

'But why should I not go there too? I will help you with your calves.'

He laughed harshly. 'You are a lady.'

'I am a servant-girl out of place,' she said with a faint smile.

'They drink and swear and curse and fight, where I go,' he growled.

'No, Richard—you go to no place that is bad. Where you go I will go also.'

He did not look in her face; he could hardly have resisted the appeal, had he done so, her face was so full of earnestness, so pale and anxious, so humble, and the eyes so full of tears. Perhaps he knew that he could not resist, were he to meet her eyes, so he kept his own averted. But the tones of her voice thrilled him, and made his head spin. He bit the end of his whip, with his brows knitted. He knew her great eyes, those lovely eyes that went through him when he met them, were fixed on him; but he would not turn towards them; his face became more frozen and drawn.

'You,' he said—by her Christian name he would not call her—you—understand me. I am not Richard to you. You must speak of me and address me as Mr. Cable.'

'But—I am your wife.'

'No,' he said; 'that is all past and for ever done with. For a little while, and then the

tie was torn away by yourself. You are coming
with me into Cornwall, to St. Kerian. There
you will live as you like. If you want money,
you shall have it; but you shall not live there
as my wife, but as Miss Cornellis, or by any
other name you like to assume. My mother
will see you want nothing; you shall not live
in my house; you will be a stranger there;
but my mother—and I, yes, and I, will know
how you are, what you do, and that you do
not again fall into evil company, and run the
risk of——'

'Of what? I ran no risk.'

'No,' he said; 'you ran no risk. No. You
are proud, proud as Satan; and yet Satan, for
all his pride, fell.'

The tears which had formed in her eyes
rolled over her cheeks. The disappointment
was very great. She had hoped that he was
going to take her back to himself. 'You need
have no fear for me,' she said in a voice half
choked with her tears; 'I have that in me
which will always hold me true and upright.
Not pride; O no, not pride—that is broken
long ago, ever since I found I had driven you
away.'

'What is it?' Still he did not look at her,
but he turned his ear attentively towards her.
She might have seen, had not her eyes been so

dim with salt, that a nerve down the side of his face from the temple was twitching.

'It is, that I love you,' she answered in a low, faint voice, but little above a whisper.

Then he stamped on the sanded floor of the village inn parlour, and clenched his hands, and stood up, and shook himself, like a great hairy dog when it leaves the water. 'Ha, ha!' he laughed; 'as of old, to patronise and play with, and then break to pieces, as a child loves its doll. I will have none of your love. I have tasted it, and it is sour.'

'Richard!'

He struck the table. 'I am not Richard— to you. That is part of your grand condescending ways. You shall call me Mr. Cable. Who knows!—in time you may come to look up to me, when I am rich and esteemed. Mr. Cable of Red Windows, Esquire.' Then he went forth tossing his shoulders, and he put on his hat in a hot and impatient way.

A struggle ensued in Josephine's bosom. It was hard for her to go down into a strange country and there live, in the same village with her husband, without being acknowledged by him, divided by all England from her own friends. He was asking too much of her, putting her through too sharp an ordeal; and yet, after a little boil up of her old pride and wilfulness, she bent to his decision. It was not for her to rebel. She had wrought the dis-union that had subsisted between them; she had made the great change in him; and she must submit, and suffer and wait, till he took her back. She must accept his terms, not impose terms of her own.

She was at the station at the time appointed, and Richard handed her a second-class ticket to Exeter. He travelled in the van with his calves, and she saw nothing of him till their arrival. Then he came to the carriage door, called a cab, shouldered her box himself, and limped with it to the carriage. 'To the Clarendon,' he said, shut the door, and climbed on the box.

On reaching the inn, an old-fashioned hotel, looking out on the close with its great trees and gray cathedral, he descended, let her out of the cab, and preceding her, ordered the waiter to let her have a room. 'The lady—she is, mind you, a real lady—she must have a good room, and a capital supper, and a fire, and be made comfortable.—Don't you stare at me as if I had aught of concern with her. I'm a common man, a cattle-jobber; but I'm charged to see after her, and that she be well attended to, as a real well-born lady, full of education and high-class manners. As for me, I put up

elsewhere—at the " Goat and Compasses,"
down by the iron bridge. I'll come in the
morning and fetch her away. It is my duty,
set me by them as are responsible for her, to
see that she be cared for and made comfortable.'
Then he went away.

Josephine was given a well-furnished bedroom, with a large window, looking out on the
elms and grass and old towers. Her box was
in the room ; and she opened it, and drew from
it some little things she needed. Then she
bathed her face, and seated herself by the window, looking out into the quiet close. The
bells of the cathedral were ringing for afternoon
service, deep-toned musical bells. The autumn
had touched the leaves and turned them. The
swallows were clustering on the gray lead roof
of the minster, arranging for migration. There
was coolness in the air ; but it was not too
chilly for Josephine to sit at the open window,
looking at the trees and listening to the bells.
She felt very lonely, more lonely than at
Bewdley. There she had the association
with old Miss Otterbourne to take off the
edge of her sense of solitude ; but now she
had no one. She was with her husband, yet
far removed from him. She was associated
with him without association. It was better to
be separated altogether, than to be in his pre-

sence daily without reciprocation. She drew her wedding-ring from her bosom and looked at it. The night before she had put it on, and had hesitated whether to wear it again; but had rehung it round her neck, determined to wait another day and see what her husband's wishes and intentions and behaviour to her were, before she did so. And now, as she looked sorrowfully at the golden hoop, she knew that it must continue to hang as before; he had forbidden her to acknowledge her tie to him and to wear his name.

How strange is the perversity of the human heart! She had married Richard without loving him; and now that she had lost him, she loved him. Her love had started up out of her anguish over her wrong done him. He had loved her when she had only highly esteemed him; and now she loved him when he despised her.

She knelt by her box, and looked over her little treasures. They were few. Her bullfinch she had not brought away; she had given it to the housemaid who had cleaned her room. She turned over her few clothes in the box and unfolded Richard's blue handkerchief In a cardboard box was the bunch of everlastings. They were now very dry, but they retained their shape and colour. 'Everlastings!' she said, and recalled the night in the deserted cottage, when she asked the rector whether he was looking up at the everlastings. ' To the Everlasting,' he had answered, and she had not understood him; but she remembered the scene and the words he had used.

The cathedral bells had ceased, and across the close came the sounds of music—the roll of the organ and the voices of the choir. Josephine closed her box and locked it, and went back to the window and listened to the soothing strains. Then, drawn as by an irresistible attraction, she went downstairs, and crossed the close, and entered the side door of the cathedral. She did not go far; she made no attempt to enter the choir, but seated herself in the aisle on the stone seat that ran along the wall. The evening light shone through the great west window, and filled the upper portion of the nave with a soft yellow glow. Below were the gray pillars and cool gray shadow. There were few loungers in the nave, and she was quite unnoticed. Her love of music made her always susceptible to its influence. The effect of the sacred music in the great Gothic minster on Josephine, in her then state of depression, was great: it soothed her mind; it was like a breath on a wound, lulling the pain and cooling the fever.

For long there had been in Josephine a craving for help, for something, or rather some one whom she could lay hold of and lean on. It was this want in her which had driven her to take Richard Cable, in defiance of her father's wishes and of the opinion of the world. Richard had failed her, and she had cast herself into a sphere in which she was as solitary and lacking assistance as much as in that she had occupied before. And now, once again, she was torn out of that sphere, and was about to be cast—she knew not where, among—she knew not what companions—and again she was without support.

She sat with her head bowed and her hands clasping her bosom, listening to the music. Her soul was bruised and aching, like the body that has been jolted and beaten. But the hurt body is cast on a bed and sleeps away its pains. Where is the bed of repose on which the weary suffering spirit can stretch itself and be recruited? Josephine was not thinking at all; she was feeling, conscious of want and weariness, of a void and pain. The aisle in which she was, was on the north side of the church; and quite in shadow, only in the beautiful vault of the nave, with its reed-like spreading ribs, hung a halo of golden haze; and in that golden haze the sweet music seemed

to thrill and throb, and send down waves of
aerial balm.

The pain in Josephine's heart became more
acute, and she bent on one side and rested her
elbow on the stone seat and put her hand to
her heart and breathed laboriously. The atti-
tude gave her some ease; and as she half
reclined thus, the waves of golden light and
angelic music swept over her, softly, gently,
as the warm sea-waves used to glide in over
the low Essex coast. Presently, Josephine slid
down on her knees and laid her head on the
cold stone seat. Then only did the meaning
of the rector come clear to her, when he
dropped an *s* as she spoke of the everlastings,
and he answered her, that he looked to the
Everlasting.

## CHAPTER L.

### BOOTS AGAIN.

NEXT morning, Josephine found a cab awaiting her. Cable had paid her bill and sent the conveyance for her. He had given instructions to the driver to convey her along the Okehampton and Launceston road beyond the town to a point where, at the head of the first hill, stood a fragment of an old stone cross. She had fancied that he would have come with his van of calves into the cathedral yard, drawn up before the Clarendon Hotel, and had her box laden on the van there; but Richard Cable had too much delicacy under his roughness of manner to subject her to such a humiliation; she was to leave the Clarendon as she had come to it, in a hired conveyance, and as a lady; only when beyond the town would he receive her box and her on his van.

She reached the cross before him, and dismounted. When she opened her purse, the driver objected—he had already received his fare. The man who had ordered him had paid. Josephine had her box placed by the side of the road. A little inn stood near the cross, and the landlady good-naturedly asked her to step in—·if she were waiting for the coach. 'No charge, miss; you needn't take anything.'

'Thank you,' said Josephine modestly; 'you are very kind; but I am not going by the coach. A gentleman—I mean a man who drives a van of calves, is going to pick me up.'

'Oh, you mean Dicky Cable. He often goes by our way.'

'Yes; I am going on with Mr. Cable.' As she spoke, she saw the cob, and Cable limping at its side, ascending the red road cut between banks of red sandstone hung with ferns and overarched with rich limes.

'He looks very greatly changed,' said Josephine to herself—'oldened, hardened, and somewhat lame.'

Presently he came up. Rain had fallen in the night, and the red mud was splashed about his boots and the wheels of the van. The calves within put their noses between the bars and lowed; they were frightened by the motion of the vehicle; but they were not hungry, for they had been fed by Cable before starting.

He scarcely said good-morning to Josephine;
it was mumbled, but he touched his hat to her.
Then he shouldered her travelling-box and put
it on the top of the van. This van consisted
of a sort of pen or cage on wheels; the sides
and top were constructed like a cage, with
bars of wood, and between the bars the air
got to the calves, and the calves were visible.
There was a seat in front, and the door into
the pen was behind—it let down so as to form
an inclined plane, up and down which the
calves could walk, when driven into or out of
the cage.

How was Josephine to be accommodated
in such a contrivance? Was she to go into
the cage among the calves, or to be slung
under the conveyance between the wheels, or
to be perched on the top, as in an omnibus?
Richard pointed with his whip to the driver's
seat.

'Am I to sit there?' she asked.—He nodded.

'Then where do you sit?'

He got upon the shaft, as a carter perches
himself.

'I do not like to take your place,' said
Josephine. 'You will be very uncomfortable
there.'

'It is not the first time you have made me
uncomfortable. Sit where I have put you. I

must be off every few minutes when we come
to a hill ; then I walk.'

That was—he limped. His thigh was well,
but he never could walk with it as formerly.
It gave him no pain, and his movements were
not ungainly, but there was a decided limp as
he walked.

He was not in a mood for conversation.
Josephine could touch him as he sat at her
feet on the shaft with his back to her. He did
not once look round : he went about his work,
driving, walking, attending to the calves, as if
he were quite alone. Nevertheless, he must
have thought of her, for when he came to a
piece of road newly stoned, he went leisurely,
and glanced furtively behind—not at her face
—to see that the jolting did not hurt her ; and
when a shower came on, without a word he
threw his waterproof coat over her knees.
Presently they came to a long ascent. He got
down and walked. She also descended and
walked on the other side from him. She
wondered whether his silence would continue
the whole way, whether he would relax his
sternness.

The journey was tedious ; the cob travelled
slowly, and the stoppages were long, whilst
farmers haggled with Richard over the price of
the calves. The sale of these latter did not,

however, begin till the road left the red sand-
stone and approached Dartmoor. The yeomen
and farmers in proximity to the moor were a
thriving race; they could send any number of
young cattle to run on the moor at a nominal
fee to the 'moormen'—that is, to certain fellows who had the privilege to guard the vast
waste of rock and down, of mountain and
valley, under the Prince of Wales as Duke of
Cornwall; for Dartmoor forest is duchy property though situated in Devon, and indeed
occupying its heart. To the present day, it is
about the borders of the moor that the old
yeoman is still to be found, occupying in many
cases his ancestral farm, the buildings of which
date back three or four hundred years. They
consist of a large quadrangle; one side is occupied by the dwelling-house, that looks into the
yard, but is divided from it by a small raised
garden. The major portion of the yard or
court is a pen for the half-wild cattle driven in
from the moor; and about it are the stables
and cow-houses, the 'shippen,' and the 'linneys'
—the 'shippen' for sheep, and the 'linneys'
for waggons and carts and the farmer's gig.

The worst seasons do not affect the yeomen
round the moor; they must thrive, when they
have free run for any number of sheep and
cattle and horses over the downs, where the

grass is always sweet, the water pure, and where disease never makes its appearance. All they have to concern themselves about is a supply of winter-food for the stock. Elsewhere, the depression in agriculture, the repeal of the corn-laws, killed off the yeomen; only on the moor fringes do they thrive to this day as sturdy, as well-to-do, and as independent, and, it must be added, as delighting in law as of old. Dartmoor lay on the south and east, and the cold clay land of North Devon on the west; land also, as already said, that is excellent running and rearing ground for young cattle. Consequently, Richard Cable, as soon as he reached the frontiers of these two poor lands—one peat, and the other clay—found buyers, but not buyers who were ready to part with their money without a haggle over coppers.

It was not Richard who went after the farmers with his goods, as a chapman goes about among farmhouses with his wares; but the yeomen and farmers came to him. But when they came, they made poor pretences that they had chanced on him when bound elsewhere, or were at the tavern for some other purpose. The times of Richard's arrival were pretty well known. The van travelled slower than the news, as the thunder rolls after the flash. The men who came after calves were

all alike in this—they had very red faces, and
all filled their clothes to overflow. They had
all loud and cheery voices, and a breezy good-
humour not unmixed with bluster, bred of the
consciousness that their pockets were well lined,
and that they were petty lords on their own
domains. In one thing, they, moreover, were
all deficient—in the knowledge of the value of
time. Josephine looked on with wonder at
the business Richard did and at the way in which
it was done. The scenery was lovely, so lovely
that she enjoyed it in spite of the trouble in
which she was. The ranges of tors, or granite
peaks of the moor, its wildness and barrenness,
contrasted with the richness of the country at
its feet; now clothed in the many-tinted gar-
ment of autumn, gray desolation towering above
pillowy woods of gold and amber, of copper
and of green. What could be more beautiful?
In her present weariness of expectation and
disappointment, she longed to fly to the re-
cesses of the moor, build herself a cell there of
lichened granite stones, and there spend the
rest of her days away from the sight and
sounds of men.

At noon on the first day, the van halted at
a small wayside inn, and Richard ordered dinner.
'There is but ham and eggs,' he said. 'Your
ladyship must put up with that to-day. The

ale is bad, but you shall have tolerable ginger-beer.'

The night was spent at an old coaching-inn, a large, rambling place with vast stables. There she was treated to an excellent supper and to the best of rooms; but Richard did not sup with her, or indeed see her after their arrival at the inn.

Next morning he paid the account, and they started on their further course. Her boots had been well cleaned; not so those of Cable, which still bore the red mud splashes that had come on them when they were in the sand-stone district.

It was now clear to Josephine that Richard would not agree to a reconciliation; she must abandon the hopes she had entertained that he would unbend and yield. She also had made up her mind; and when they came to a hill, up which both walked, she went to him on his side of the horse. 'Mr. Cable,' she said, 'you are at once kind and cruel. You provide for me very differently than for yourself, and make provision that I shall lack no comfort; but you do not give me a good word, and not a look good or bad.'

'Well,' said he, 'of whom have I learned to be cruel? You were scornful and offensive because I did not in a few weeks acquire your ways; and now I am better, I have learned something—that you have taught me—to be unfeeling and seek my own self-interest.'

'No; I was never either one or the other.'

He laughed contemptuously. 'Not unfeeling!'

'No, Richard—I mean, Mr. Cable—I was thoughtless, but not unfeeling. I was not self-seeking, or I would not have married you.'

'You married me to suit a whim; and when you had me, the whim came to slap me in the face and sneer at my manners.'

She drew a long sigh; there was truth in this, and she did not contradict it.

'But we will not cry over spilt milk and strive to patch up broken eggs. The thing is done and sealed up and stowed away in the lockers of the past.'

'Tell me this, Richard: are you so set against me in your own mind that you will not take me to your side again? Are we never to come nearer each other than as I sit on the box, and you on the shaft, with your back turned to me? Is your face always to look away from me?'

'For ever and for ever. It is your doing.'

'I have trespassed against you, I know; but I suppose to all who trespass, forgiveness is due when sought with tears.'

'No,' he said; 'your trespass was too deep.'

'And I am to be for ever separated from
you?'

'For ever.'

'Then—Mr. Cable, if I am not to be regarded as a wife, I will owe you nothing. I
have money, and I will pay for my lodging and
food at the inns. I will not be indebted to
you for anything. What had you determined
on for me at St. Kerian?'

'I also have money; I will not let you
want. You shall have all you need to live like
a lady; you shall have a house and a servant;
and you shall have half of all the money I earn,
and I earn now a great deal.'

'I will not touch it—no, not a penny of it.'

'You are proud,' he said, scowling—'proud
and wilful; headstrong always.'

'And you are proud, Mr. Cable. There is
the fortune of Cousin Gabriel Gotham, your
father, lying untouched; the rents and divi-
dends are accumulating. You will not have
them, and I will not. Yes, you are proud, and
I am proud also. I have some spirit left in me,
though much is gone. I will live at St. Kerian,
as that is your wish; but I will not share your
earnings—I will not touch any of it. I will
work for my own bread, and not eat that of
charity. I have a little money. Good Miss
Otterbourne forced a five-pound note on me,

and I have saved my wages. I will buy myself
a sewing-machine, and live at St. Kerian by my
own hands and feet. I suppose there is sufficient
vanity among the girls there to make them desire to dress beyond their station; and that the
Government schools have done their work
effectually in giving them a distaste for doing
their own needlework. So there will be an
opportunity for me to pick up a livelihood, and
to be indebted to none—to you, least of all.'

'Proud,' he muttered—'proud and way-
ward, as of old. I feed my calves. Why should
not I feed you?'

'Because I am not a calf.'

They walked on in silence some way.
Josephine's blood was roused. After reaching
the top of the hill, before mounting, she said in
a less excited and resolute tone: 'Do not call
me wrong-headed. I have my self-respect to
sustain, and I cannot live on your charity if I
may not bear your name.'

Again they drove on some little way—now
over a down that commanded a glorious view
of rolling land stretching far away to the west
and north-west, and of rugged granite peaks;
their sides strewn with overturned rocks,
divided from each other by clefts, out of which
rushed brawling torrents, coffee-coloured with

the dye of the peat-bogs out of which they sprung.

When they came to another rise, Josephine dismounted again and walked up the hill beside her husband. The hill was steep, and she walked bent forward, looking at the ground. 'Mr. Cable,' she said, 'at the inn where we spent the night, my boots were cleaned, but not yours.'

'No,' he answered, with a short laugh. 'I was not there as a grand gentleman traveller, but as a plain trading wayfarer. They don't black the boots of such as me.'

'They are plastered with mud of many colours.'

'Does it offend you that your driver has dirty boots, my lady?'

'No, Mr. Cable; but I think it would be pleasanter for yourself, if your boots were cleaned.'

'My boots! I remember what offence they gave you once. They would not take a polish. They were so steeped in oil that they might not come into your ladyship's boudoir! Are you sneering at my boots again?'

'No, Richard; I never sneer now.' She put her delicate hand over her brow and wiped it, and then got up into her place again.

Presently they came to a spring that gushed

into a granite trough—a spring of such crystalline brightness, that looking down through the water was like looking through a magnifying-glass. There was a button at the bottom of the trough, and one could distinguish the four holes in it.

'This water is very good and fresh; shall I give you some?' asked Richard Cable.

'No,' answered Josephine. 'I will take nothing from you, not even a cup of cold water. I will help myself. I will take nothing till it is offered in love.'

He looked hastily at her, and saw that her eyes were full of tears. He trembled, and lashed his horse savagely, and uttered something much like an oath. He was angry with the cob—it was going to sleep over its journey; and a horse that goes to sleep whilst walking is liable to fall and cut his knees. Richard Cable detected, or fancied he detected, somnolency in the horse, and he worried it with whip and jerk of rein till he had roused it to full activity and a trot, whereat all the calves began to low and plead not to be so severely shaken; but Cable had no compassion on the calves; he lashed into the horse, and made him run along as he had not run that day or last.

'It is all pride and wilfulness,' he said to himself.

K 2

From sitting on the shaft with his legs hanging down, they were much splashed with mud by the horse, as he went through every wet and dirty place in the road; this was especially the case when he was trotting; and Richard, looking down at his boots, saw them caked with mud, layer on layer, or clot on clot; below was the red, then the white mud of the pounded granite, then the brown of loamy land, then black from peat-water, where the road traversed the down.

'They are a bit unsightly,' he said to himself. 'And when I come to Sticklepath, where I put up for the night, I'll mind and have them dried over the fire in the kitchen; and I'll clean them myself in the morning. She's right—one ought to keep one's-self respectable.'

When they reached the place called Sticklepath, a hamlet with an inn, and a chapel whitewashed and thatched with straw, and looking like a cottage, he ordered supper, and then went after his cob, to rub him down with straw. He was careful of his beast, and always attended to his comforts and necessities himself. Then he got milk for the calves; but when he came out into the yard, he found Josephine there with a pan of skimmed milk, dipping in her hand and holding it to the hungry creatures, who opened their pink wet mouths and mumbled her hand till they had sucked off it all the milk.

'How proud she is!' muttered Cable. 'She does this out of wickedness—to pay me for having given her a lift in my van. She will owe me nothing.'

Before he went to bed, he took his boots to the kitchen and asked that they might be put where they would dry before morning, when he would brush them over himself. He slept soundly that night; and on waking, dressed himself, brushed the mud off the bottoms of his trousers, and then descended in his stocking-soles in quest of his boots. As he came down the back-stairs, he could look into and across the kitchen, and he saw behind it, in the back-shed that served the purpose of boothole and back kitchen, the figure of Josephine. She stood near the door, with the fresh morning light streaming in on her, and white pigeons flying about outside, and perching near the door, expecting the morning largess of crumbs. She had her sleeves turned back, exposing her beautiful arms, and—she was blackening his boots.

## CHAPTER LI.

### ISHTAR.

RICHARD CABLE reascended the stairs unheard and unseen. He was irritated at what he had observed. 'How proud she is!' he said. 'There is no breaking her stubborn spirit. She does this to pay me for her carriage.'

It is a curious fact that we are prone to note and condemn in others the vice that mars our own selves. We are always keen-sighted with respect to the mote in our brother's eye, especially when it is a chip off the beam in our own eye. I have known a woman, who was a mischief-maker with her tongue throughout a neighbourhood, declare that of all things she abhorred was gossip, and that, therefore, she avoided So-and-so as a scandal-monger. The conceited man turns up his already cocked nose at another prig; and the talker is impatient of the love of chatter in his friend. I once knew two exceedingly talkative men who monopolised the whole conversation at table. The one

invited the other to make a walking expedition
with him of a month; but they returned in
three days. 'I could not stand B,' said A; 'I
was stunned with his tongue.'—'I refused to go
on with A,' said B; 'he talked me lame.' The
girl who sings flat, criticises the lack of tune in
a companion; and the man who paints badly is
the first to detect the blemishes in another's picture; and I am quite sure my most severe
critics will be those who have written the worst
novels.

Richard Cable was convinced that Josephine
was proud and self-willed; and everything she
did, every act of submission, every gentle appeal
for forgiveness, was viewed by him through the
distorted medium of his own pride. Indistinctly,
he perceived that she was asking him to be
received back on his terms—that she was ready
to make every sacrifice for this end; but he
could not or would not believe that she was
acting from any other motive than caprice. Her
pride was hurt because he had left her, and she
sought to recover him, not because she cared
for him, certainly not because she would be
more considerate of him, but to salve over her
wounded self-love.

An uneducated man, when he gets an idea
into his head, will not let it go. He hugs it, as
the Spartan lad hugged the fox though it bit

into his vitals. There is no rotation of crops in his brain. The idea once planted there, grows and spreads, and eats up all the nutriment, and overshadows the whole surface, and allows nothing to grow under it, like the beech, which poisons the soil beneath its shadow with its dead leaves and mast cases. A man who has undergone culture puts into his head one idea, and as soon as it is ripe, reaps and garners it, ploughs up the soil, puts in another of a different nature —never lets his brain be idle, and never gives it up permanently to one idea or set of ideas. Or rather—his head is an allotment garden, in which no single idea occupies the entire field, but every lobe is used for a different crop, precisely as in an allotment every variety of vegetable is grown.

Now, Richard Cable had had the idea of Josephine's haughtiness so ploughed into his mind that he could harbour no other idea. It grew and spread like a weed, and poisoned the soil of his mind, so that no wholesome plants, no sweet herbs could flourish there. It overmastered, it outgrew, it strangled all the fragrant and nutritious plants that once occupied that garden-plot. Its roots ran like those of an ash through every portion, and spread over the entire subsoil, that nothing else could grow there, or could only grow in a stunted and starved condition. So, with singular perversity, Cable resented the conduct of Josephine in cleaning his boots, and he attributed her act to unworthy motives. He said not a word about his boots till the van was in motion, and he started up the steep hill. Then he exclaimed : ' Whatever have these folk at the inn been about with my boots, that they shine like those of a dancing-master ? ' Then he went through a puddle, and came out with them tarnished and begrimed. He did not look round at Josephine, who made no remark, but next morning cleaned his boots again. After that, Cable kept them in his bedroom. He would not have them cleaned by Josephine.

All the calves were disposed of before Launceston was reached ; and as the load was light, the horse rattled on with the van at a better rate. When they drew near to St. Kerian, Cable said : ' I have written beforehand to my mother, and told her my intentions. She will have arranged lodgings for you, where you may stay on your arrival. After that, as you are wilful, you must suit yourself ; but I could not drop you from the van in the street with nowhere to go to. Even the calves are not treated thus ; each goes to its allotted cowhouse. I have told my mother to engage the lodging as for an acquaintance of hers—

acquaintance, understand, not friend—and to pay a month in advance.'

'That,' said Josephine, 'I will not allow.' She opened her purse. 'What has been spent, I will refund.'

'I do not know what the sum is,' said Cable angrily. 'I insist on paying this. Afterwards, pay as you will.'

'I will not allow it,' said Josephine vehemently. 'No; indeed, indeed I will not. If you choose to acknowledge me, then I will take anything from you, and be thankful for every crumb of bread and drop of water; but if you will not, then I will set my teeth and lips, and not a crumb of bread or drop of water of your providing shall pass between them.'

'Yourself—yourself still; wilful, defiant, proud!' he said, with a frown and a furtive glance at her over his shoulder. Then he shouted rather than spoke: 'Why will you not enjoy the estate and money bequeathed to you? It is yours; no one will dispute it with you.'

'I will not touch it,' answered Josephine, 'because I have no right to it.'

'You have every right: it was left to you.'

'But it ought never to have come to me. It was properly, justly yours.'

'I will not have it!' shouted Richard. 'You know that. I am too proud to take it.'

'And I also; I am too proud to take it.'

'We are both proud, are we? Flint and steel, we strike, and the sparks fly. It will be ever so—strike, strike, and the sparks fly.'

'When I reach St. Kerian,' said Josephine, 'I suppose, if you continue in this unforgiving mind, I shall see nothing of you?'

'Nothing.'

'It is hard to put me there alone, without friends, a stranger.'

'I came there a stranger, and have now no friends there.'

'But you have your children. With them you need no outsiders; but I am quite alone. You will let me see the dear little ones?'

'No,' he answered; 'I will not let them come near you lest they take the infection.'

'Richard,' said Josephine very sadly, and in a low despondent voice, 'it seems to me that we have exactly altered our positions; I was once full of cruel speeches and unkind acts, and you bore them with singular patience. Now, it is you who are cruel and unkind, and I do not cry out, though you cause me great pain.'

He did not answer her; but he said: 'I will not be seen driving you into St. Kerian, as I would not be seen driving you out of Exeter. You shall get out at this next inn.

It is respectable and clean. You shall stay the night there, and to-morrow come on with the carrier's waggon.'

'Will there be no one to receive me and show me where I am to go? O Richard! you are treating me very cruelly.'

'I am treating you as you deserve,' he answered. 'My mother shall await your arrival and show you to your lodging.'

He drew up before the tavern that stood by itself where roads crossed. He took down her box and then something else from the inside of the van.

'What is this?' asked Josephine. 'It is not mine; but it has "Cornellis, passenger, St. Kerian," on it; and—it—it looks like a sewing-machine.'

'It is a sewing-machine.'

She stood and looked at him. 'You mean it as a present for me. You bought it in Launceston, because I said I would work as a dress-maker and so earn my livelihood.—No; I will not take anything you give me: send it back.'

He stamped with impatience. 'How perverse and proud you are!—You do not alter; you are always the same. I do not give you the sewing-machine. My poor little crippled Bessie shall give it you. Each of my children has a savings-bank book, and for every journey

I make, some of the profits go into their little
stores. Bessie shall pay for the sewing-machine
out of her money. It shall be withdrawn from
the bank for the purpose.—Will that content
you?'

Josephine thought a moment, and then,
raising her great full eyes on him, she said:
'Yes; I will take it from Bessie—Richard! if,
as you assert, I was the cause of her being
injured, yet I am very sure her gentle little
heart bears me no malice. You have told her
that I crippled her, you have taught her to
hate me——'

'No,' answered Cable hurriedly; 'I have
not spoken of you, not uttered your name since
I left Hanford. The children have forgotten
your existence.'

'Let little Bessie come to me and I will
tell her all. I will take to myself the full
blame, and then—she will put her dear arms
round my neck and kiss me and forgive me.
But you——'

'But I,' interrupted Cable, 'am not a child.
Bessie does not know the consequences, cannot
measure the full amount of injury done her.
If she could, she would never, never forgive
you; no '—he broke his stick in his vehemence
—' never! If she had a head to understand,
she would say: "There are hours every day

that I suffer pain. I cannot sleep at night
because of my back. That woman is the cause.
I cannot run about and play with my sisters.
That woman did it. I shall grow up deformed,
and people will turn and laugh at me, and rude
children point and mock me. That woman
brought this upon me. I shall see my sisters
as young maidens, beautiful and admired, only
I shall not be admired. That woman is the
cause. I shall love with all the fire of my
heart, that grows whilst my body remains
stunted, my woman's heart in a child's frame
—but no one will love me; he whom I love
will turn from me in disgust and take another
in his arms. I owe that also to this woman."
—If she foresaw all this, would Bessie forgive
you and love you, and put her arms about you
and kiss you? No; she would get up on her
knees on your lap and beat your two great
eyes with her little fists till you could not see
out of them any more, but wept out of them
brine and blood.' Then he mounted the
driver's seat in front of his van, lashed the
horse, and left her standing in the road before
the inn with her box and the sewing-machine.

Thereupon, a strong temptation arose and
beset Josephine. Why should she go on to
St. Kerian?—why sojourn there as a stranger,
ignored by her own husband? Why should

she bow to a life of privation of the most trying
kind, intellectual privation, if nothing was to be
gained by it? She had reached the first shelf
in her plunge, and the golden cup was not
there. Now, she was diving to a second and
lower shelf, and she saw no prospect of retriev-
ing what she sought on it. The shelf on which
she had first lodged was in shallow water,
within the light of the sun; it was not so far
removed from the social and spiritual life of the
cultured class to which she belonged, as that
into which she was now called to descend. On
that other shelf there was ebb and flow, and
now and then she could enjoy the society of
her social equals, if not to converse with them,
to hear their cultured voices, see their ease of
manner, and enjoy the thousand little amenities
of civilisation which hang about the mansion of
a lady of position. She had been there as a
mermaid belonging to both regions, half lady,
half servant; and very unpleasant, not to say
repugnant to her cultured instincts and moral
sense, as she had found the lower element
which had half engirdled her, there was still an
upper region in which she could breathe. Now
she was to be wholly submerged, to go down
to the depth where only the unlettered and
undisciplined swim, where only broad dialect is
spoken, coarse manners are in vogue, and life

is without any of the polish and adornment found in the world above the water-line. In the upper air, when she floated, she could hear the birds sing and see the flowers, and smell the fragrance of the clover and bean fields; below, she would hear nothing but strident tones, see nothing but forms uncouth, smell nothing but what is rank. Why should she make this second plunge? Why—when she clearly saw that on this lower platform the golden goblet did not lie? Would it be a final leap? Would it necessitate a further descent into gulfs of darkness and horror? No; hardly that. Intellectually, there was no further dive. She could hardly find a ledge below that of the unreasoning, unread, untrained. 'Neath that was the abyss of moral defect, into which she could not fall.

In the old Assyrian poem of 'Ishtar,' the goddess is represented descending through several houses into Hades, and as she approaches each, the gatekeepers divest her of some of her clothing, till she reaches Abadon, where she is denuded of everything. Josephine was something like Ishtar—she was forced in her downward pilgrimage, at every mansion of the nether world, to lay aside some of her ornaments acquired above. She had set forth with her mind richly clothed; she was a refined and accomplished girl, passionately fond of music, with a delicate artistic taste, a love of literature, and an eager mind for the revelations of science. If she had an interest that came second to music, it was love of history—that faculty which, like music and colour, is inherent in some, is wholly deficient in others. To some, the present is but a cut flower, of fleeting charm, unless it have its root in the past, when at once it acquires interest, and is tenderly watched and cultivated. The historic faculty is closely allied to the imagination. It peoples a solitude with forms of beauty and interest; it builds up walls, and unrolls before the fancy the volume of time, full of pictures. The possessor of these gifts is never alone, for the past is always about him, a past so infinitely purer and better than the present, because sublimated in the crucible of the mind.

Now, what struck Josephine above everything in the under-water world into which she stepped was the inability of its denizens to appreciate what is historical. They seemed to her like people who have no perspective, like half-blind men, who see men as trees walking. They had no clear ideas as to time or as to distance. Brussels and Pekin, foreign cities about equidistant, and Iceland and Tierra del Fuego, foreign islands in the same hemisphere.

The Romans built the village churches; but whether the classic Romans or the Roman Catholics, was not at all known: nor was it certain when Oliver Cromwell stabled his horses in the churches, whether in the time of the Romans, or in the Chartist rows; neither whether Oliver Cromwell were a French republican or an Irish papist. Turkeys came of course from Turkey, of which, probably, Dorking is the capital, because thence came also some big fowls; and necessarily Jerusalem artichokes are derived from the holy city, or else why are they called Jerusalem artichokes? In literature it was the same. Below the water, the denizens had heard of Shakspeare, but didn't think much of him; he didn't come near Miss Braddon. Swift—yes, he wrote children's stories—'Gulliver's Travels' and the 'Robins.' Thackeray! he was nowhere—not fit to hold a candle to Mrs. Henry Wood; there were no murders in his tales. In this subaqueous world, music was not; if there had been stillness it would have been well; but in place of the exquisite creations of the great tone masters, sprang a fungoid, scabrous growth of comic song, 'Villikens and his Dinah,' 'Pop goes the Weasel,' and revivalist hymns. Josephine in descending so low left behind her everything that to her made life worth having.

She must cast aside her books, lay down her music, her painting; and be cut away from all communion with the class in which all the roots of her inner life were planted. Was she called on to do this? What would come of the venture?

But then came another question: Could she go back? To Hanford Hall and to her father? No; she had taken her course with full determination of pursuing it to the end. She would not return. She must follow what her heart told her was the right thing to do, at whatever cost to herself. Ishtar would lay aside every adornment, only not the pure white robe of her moral dignity. Before the last house, she would stand and wait, and not tap at that door, wait, and lie down there and die, rather than return except at the call of Richard.

.

# CHAPTER LII.

### THE SECOND SHELF.

Mrs. Cable was waiting before the door of the St. Kerian inn, where hung the sign of the 'Silver Bowl,' when Josephine arrived. She received her with stately gravity and some coldness. The old woman saw that her daughter-in-law was greatly altered. Her girlishness was gone; womanhood had set in, stamping and characterising her features. She was thin and pale, and did not look strong.

Mrs. Cable led her to the village grocer and postmistress, a Miss Penruddock, and showed Josephine a couple of neat plain rooms, one above-stairs, a bedroom, and the other below as a sitting-room. Everything was scrupulously clean; the walls were whitewashed, the bed and window-furniture white, the china white, and the deal boards of the floor scrubbed as white as they could be got. Josephine's box was moved upstairs, and the sewing-machine put in the parlour below. Her landlady was in and out for some little while, to make sure that all was comfortable, till the sorting-time for the letters engaged her in the shop. The atmosphere of the house was impregnated with the odour of soap, tea, and candles—a wholesome and not unpleasant savour.

Bessie Cable remained standing in the bedroom; her tall form looked unnaturally tall in the low room, of which the white ceiling was only seven feet above the white floor. ' Is there anything further you require?' she asked. ' I promised my son that I would see that you were supplied with every requisite.'

Josephine looked at her, and drew beseechingly towards her, with her arms out, pleading to be taken to the old woman's heart. But Bessie Cable's first thought was for her son, and she could not show tenderness where he refused recognition.

' I am sorry to receive you thus,' said Mrs. Cable; ' but I cannot forget how that you have embittered my son's life, not only to himself, but also to me, his mother. I had looked forward to a peaceful old age, with him happy, after the storms and sorrows of a rough life. But he shipwrecked his peace and mine when he took you. I dare say you are repentant. The rector told me as much; but the wrong done remains working. One year's seeds make five years' weeds, and the weeds are growing out of the sowing of your cruel lips.'

'You also!' cried Josephine. 'Is no one to be kind to me—all to reproach me?'

'You must make friends here.'

'But you—will you not be my mother, and my friend?'

'Your mother—no. Your friend!—not openly. That I cannot be, because of my son; but I will not refuse you an inner friendship. I believe that now you intend to do right, and that you have acted well in coming here.'

'You think so?'

'Yes; I am sure you have. You could in no other way have shown that you wished to undo the past.'

'I am glad you say that; oh, I am glad! Yesterday, I had a terrible moment of struggle; I was almost about to go away, and not come on here. Now you have repaid me for my fight by these words.'

Bessie looked steadily and searchingly at her. 'I have had years of waiting for what could never come. I had ever an anguish at my heart, like a cancer eating it out. But that is over. It was torn out by the roots in one hour of great struggle and pain, and since then I have been at ease within. You have now your pain. Mine was different from yours.

Mine grew out of a blow dealt me. Yours comes because you have dealt blows. There is nothing for it but to bear the pain and wait. Some day the pain will be over; but how it will be taken away God only knows. I thought that mine would never go; but it went, and went suddenly, and I have felt nothing since. No medicine can heal you—only patience. Wait and suffer; and in God's good time and in His way, the pain will be taken away.'

Josephine suddenly caught the old woman's hand and kissed it.

'Do not—do not!' exclaimed Bessie, as if frightened.

'O Mrs. Cable,' said Josephine, 'I will wait.—And now, tell me another thing. I have said that I will receive nothing of Richard till he will acknowledge me. I know I have acted very wrongly, but I think he is too unforgiving.'

'It is not for me to judge my son, nor to hear any words of condemnation from you.'

'I do not wish to condemn him; but I feel that his justice is prevailing over his mercy.'

'Who hardened him?'

'I—I did it; and I am reaping what I sowed. I own that. But, as he will not receive me, will not season anything he offers me with love, am I wrong to refuse to accept aught of him?'

Mrs. Cable did not answer immediately, but presently she said: 'No—you do right. I did the same. I would not touch anything; but then my case was different; I was the wronged, not the wrongdoer.'

'More the reason that I should refuse,' said Josephine with vehemence.

Again Mrs. Cable considered; then said: 'Yes, that stands to reason; the wrongdoer gives to the wronged one to expiate the wrong, the wrongdoer does not receive from the one wronged—that would aggravate the offence.'

'I am glad you see this,' said Josephine.— 'Now—what have you paid for my lodgings? He said you had given a month's rent in advance.'

Mrs. Cable coloured. 'You shall not pay that; indeed you shall not. I engaged the rooms.'

'Because he asked you. I will not stand in his debt.'

'I cannot receive money from you,' exclaimed Mrs. Cable. 'It would burn my fingers.'

Then Josephine knelt by her box and opened it. 'We will come to an agreement another way,' she said. 'There is something

in the bottom of my trunk—the only poor
remains of my finery I have brought with me.
You shall take that, and some day it can be
cut up or adapted for Mary. Perhaps Mary
may be married, and then she shall have my
old wedding dress. I brought it from Hanford
with me, not that I intended ever again to
wear it, but it served me as a remembrancer.
In it I was married, and in it I gave the last
offence to my husband. In it I gained him,
and in it I lost him. But I shall require it
now no more. Take it, and do with it what
you like. The silk is very good; it was a
costly dress. Richard is building a new house;
the driver pointed it out to me as I came along
—do not think he had any notion how nearly
I was interested in it—he said that Richard
Cable came poor to the place, and will soon be
the wealthiest man in it. When he has his
grand new house, his little girls must dress well
as little ladies; and Mary, when she is married
from it, may wear my wedding dress. I trust
she will be happier than I have been or am
likely to be.' She looked up from the box.
How large her eyes were, full of expression and
intelligence—beautiful eyes, and now looking
unusually bright and large because she was
tired and thin and sunken about the sockets of
the eyes.

'Have you been unwell?' asked Mrs. Cable.

'No—only unhappy.'

'It takes a great deal of unhappiness to kill,' said Bessie meditatively. 'I thought sometimes I could not live, so great were my sorrow and shame.'

'I do not care much whether I live or die,' said Josephine. 'Life is very full of trouble and disappointment, of humiliation and self-reproach to me.'—Then, in an altered voice: 'Will you take the dress?'

'Yes,' answered Mrs. Cable, still studying her face—'yes—Josephine.'

A smile played over the face of the still kneeling girl. 'It does me good to hear my Christian name again,' she said. 'At Bewdley, I was only "Cable." I should be thankful now for Joss-e-phine, though once I scorned to be so named.' She replaced her clothes in the trunk and laid the white silk dress on the bed.

'What is that? That is one of Richard's old handkerchiefs,' said Mrs. Cable.

'Yes,' answered Josephine, lowering her head. 'I found it in the cottage after you were all gone. I will do up the dress in it, if you will promise to let me have the old blue handkerchief again. I—I value it. I once laughed at it—just as I laughed at my name pronounced incorrectly, and at his boots; and now—it is otherwise. I value the handkerchief; let me have it again.'

Then Mrs. Cable took Josephine's head between her hands and drew it towards her; then checked herself, and thrust her off, and said: 'I cannot, till my son acknowledges you; it would not be just to him.'

Josephine sighed. The colour had fluttered to her cheek and her eyes had laughed; and now the colour faded and the laugh went out of her eyes. 'Am I not to see the children?' she asked.

'I cannot forbid you seeing them,' answered Bessie Cable; 'but you are not to make their acquaintance and be friendly with them. You shall make them all a new set of gowns and frocks; you shall have their old ones as patterns, but must make them a size larger, as the children are growing—that is, all but Bessie. I suppose that the dresses will have to be fitted; then you may touch them, and speak to them; but you must not kiss them or be friendly with them. Speak to them only about the fit of their clothes.'

'I am very hardly treated,' said Josephine.

'You must consider—you have brought it on yourself.'

'Yes, I have done that, and I must bear my pain.—I shall see little or nothing of Richard?'

'Little or nothing, and he will not speak to you. He is away a great deal now. We see him only at intervals; and when he is at home, he wishes to be left undisturbed with his children.' Then, once more, Mrs. Cable asked if Josephine had all that she needed; and left, with the white silk dress tied up in Richard's blue handkerchief, when assured that nothing further was required except that which she was not empowered to give.

Many days passed, and Josephine sat in her little parlour working at the frocks for the seven girls—frocks!—gowns for the elder children, who grew apace. Through her window she saw them pass, tall, beautiful maidens with fair hair, like corn, as yellow and as shining, and eyes blue, and cheeks like wild-roses. Among the dark-haired, dark-eyed, and sallow-skinned natives, they were looked at with surprise and a little envy. They kept themselves aloof from the village children —not that they were proud, not that they shared their father's prejudices, but that they had enough of companions among themselves. They were an attached family; they had been nurtured in love, and the love their father had poured into their infant hearts had filled them and overflowed towards each other. They had, indeed, their little quarrels, but they passed like April gusts, leaving the sunshine brighter after the cloud, and the landscape fresher for the shower.

Then, at times, Josephine's work fell from her fingers, and she sat with the needle in her hand, poised and motionless, looking before her. It was not the historic muse who then visited her and raised a mirage picture of castles and knights jousting, and gay ladies looking on in the most picturesque of costume; or of tapestried chambers, in which walked Van Dyck figures with long hair and Steen-kirks, and rapiers clinking and spurs jingling, and lapdogs of King Charles's breed snapping—it was a muse who is nameless, a Cinderella muse, thrust aside by her sisters, and clean forgotten, the Muse of Unfulfilled aspirations, clothed in white with a hawthorn crown, and eyes filled with tears, and bare feet dripping blood.

What were the visions raised before the brooding mind of Josephine, sitting at ease in the enchanted palace, sent to sleep and made motionless in the midst of work? The picture brought up by the magic wand of the muse was a humble one—of a little cradle, in which lay a sleeping babe, with one small hand out, and a coral resting on the quilt; of a baby snuggling into her bosom at night, and sobbing, and being patted, patted, patted by the hour, and talked to half-pitifully, half-wearily, to coax it to sleep; of a child growing up, standing at her knee and learning to thread beads, and whilst threading, repeating, ' Once upon a time, when Jenny Wren was young ; ' of a young maiden—like Mary in growth and beauty and sweetness and innocence, looked up to and loved by all the village, and adored by her mother, who only lived and thought for her. Her day-dream went no further.  Oh, if she could have had a child to love and labour for, to cherish and talk to, to kiss and laugh to and weep over !—her solitude would not have been so depressing, her pain not so unrelieved. Bessie Cable had endured years of suffering, yet what was hers to that of Josephine, for Bessie had her child to love ?  She looked for the time when the fair faces of Richard's daughters passed her window, and her ear was alert to catch every tone and inflection of their sweet voices, whenever they came into the shop to buy the groceries needed for their home.

When they came to be fitted on, her slim white fingers trembled, and she could not well see what were the defects to be remedied, because her eyes were clouded. Finally, the seven dresses were finished and sent to the cottage, and then each had a little packet of sweet things neatly wrapped up in the pocket; for that the children came and thanked Miss Penruddock, for they supposed the kind shop-keeper had put them there.

With such dear children about him, Richard had a home complete in joys, and he needed not another inmate. He could dispense with his wife, who was not the mother of these lambs; surely, he did not imagine the solitude of the girl who was without an associate of any kind.

After Josephine had done the frocks, other work came in. The servant-maids at the parsonage wanted this and that; and then some of the farmers' wives sent for her to come and work at their houses. She found that thus only could she obtain continuous work. At the farms she was well treated, given plenty of food, somewhat coarse, but wholesome, served in a rough way, and partaken with the labouring men from the land. There was also plenty of conversation going on, but it was wholly confined to local gossip—the misdoings of this young woman, the shameful conduct of the parson in preaching at So-and-so, and the favouritism of the schoolmaster among the children. The maladies of the family, of the cattle, of the ducks and hens, were discussed with intolerable prolixity, and with a breadth of language unsuitable to the narrowness of the subject. The costume of the continental peasant is a century behind the fashion of the present. The Black Forester wears the knee-breeches and long coat and waistcoat that were the dress of gentlemen in the time of our great-grandfathers; and the Tyrolean peasantess wears the short bodice of our great-grand-mothers. We have no costume in England—slopshops everywhere kill costume—but we have social habits, and the habits of our lower middle-class, of the yeomen and the tenant-farmer, are those of our great-grandfathers; they crack the same free jokes, and their wives laugh at them, as our great-grandmothers laughed; and they drink till they are merry, and upset their light carts coming home from market; and fall into the ditch, just as our great-grandfathers tumbled under their tables. The wives are thrifty, and great at cordials and supplies of linen; and they as girls had worked samplers, which they retain in married life framed on their walls, to be tokens of their skill with the needle; just as did these ancient ladies in our dining-room who look down on us out of their tarnished frames and through cracked varnish.

In the Eastern counties, the old race of small farmers and yeomen have well-nigh disappeared, or rather they bid fair to disappear, before the gentleman farmer with his thousand acres; but the agricultural depression which has cut down these big men has spared the little, and they are reappearing again. In the West of England there are very few mammoths, only small men, and the small men make the money and stand the stress of hard times.

The class among which Josephine went was quite different from that in the servants' hall at Bewdley. That class was one of the spoiled tools of luxury, young men and girls transplanted from cottages where they had lacked everything but the barely necessary, to a house where they lacked nothing, but rioted and surfeited on abundance. In their homes they had been subjected to the rough moral control of village opinion; in the hall, they were a law unto themselves. They had been brought up in freedom and frankness; and they found themselves in a region where they must practise dissimulation as part of their qualification. They resembled wild flowers brought into a forcing-house, treated with strong manures and much bottom heat. But where Josephine now went, it was among wild flowers in their natural element; they were fresh, strong, rough-stemmed; not brilliant or choice, but natural. In the servants' hall, an atmosphere of absurd affectation had prevailed : Mr. Polkinghorn talked of his ancestors; and the maids languished, minced their words, and imitated the easy motions of the ladies they saw. In the farmhouse, the fresh air blew—all was natural and hearty—but the fresh air was somewhat charged with the reek of stable and cowhouse. From the farmer down to the servant, all were blunt, dull, noisy, ignorant, free in their talk, but with a healthy downright sense of the just and moral, and with great kindliness of heart and readiness to assist one another. Josephine was obliged to carry her sewing-machine when she went to the farmhouses, scattered at considerable distances from the 'church-town' where was the post-office where she lived. As the winter drew on, the nights were dark and the weather stormy. She was often wet through and tired, and the burden of the sewing-machine was almost more than she could bear. She did not like to ask to be assisted with it; the sturdy country girls thought nothing of such a weight, and did not mind a wet through and a trudge in the mud, so that she was not volunteered assistance.

When she reached her lodgings, she was sometimes so exhausted that she flung herself on her bed, too fagged to take off her wet things; and thus she would have lain and fallen asleep, had not the kindly postmistress looked after her, and insisted on her getting up and putting on dry clothes. Every Sunday morning early, she went to the cob cottage in the lane that led to Rosscarrock, with a little basket in her hand, and laid on the window-ledge of the children's room seven little bunches of flowers—rosemary and mignonette, a monthly rose and marigold, such simple flowers as she could beg of the farmers' wives where she worked on the Saturday. And every Sunday the seven girls went to church with these flower-posies in their bosoms—'the pixy present,' they called them, and always wondered whence they came; and little thought that they came from the strange young woman with the wonderful voice, that the vicar's wife had lately taken into the choir. Did Richard guess? He asked no questions; but his mother said to him, when he happened to be home on Sundays: 'Do you see these pretty posies? The little maids found them again this morning on their window-sill. —Smell them, Richard; how sweet they are— they scent the room.'

'We shall have grand flowers when we

come to Red Windows,' he said.—'No; I will
not smell them: they give me a headache;
take them away.'

Then winter-frost killed most flowers; but
the feathery seed-heads of the traveller's joy,
with blackberry leaves of carmine and orange
and gamboge and sap-green, with a rose-hip
or two, made nosegays as beautiful and rich as
any made of flowers, and these were laid as
had been the bunches of blossom.

Christmas morning came, and Josephine
started from her bed as the day began to
break. She had made seven of the prettiest
little posies of white chrysanthemums, which
had flowered on untouched by frost, and they
were surrounded by the green fronds of the
crane's-bill.

What was that? Her heart stood still, as,
undressed, in her night-attire, with a white
bunch in each hand, and her dark hair down
her back, she stood listening. What was that?
A sound she knew well, but had not heard for
long. Again! What was it? In the room
or outside? Then a cry of joy. My Puffles!
my Puffles! You dear one! Who has brought
you here?'

Her bullfinch, in the cage, that she had
sorrowfully parted with at Bewdley, was in her
window. Who had brought it her? Who had

thought of her sorrowing to be without her bird? Who but he who had let it go and caught it again?

That Christmas Day, clear and sweet rang out the voice of Josephine in the song of the angels, and her heart beat with hope.

# CHAPTER LIII.

THE house progressed. By Christmas, the roof
was on ; then the plasterers and the carpenters
went to work, not fast, but leisurely. They
kept holiday on Christmas Day, and on Old
Christmas and at New Year ; and they knocked
off work early on Saturdays, and came to work
late on Mondays. They had much information to impart to each other, and all were
called together to consult on every detail.
When it was wet weather, they came and
looked at the work and went away ; and
charged half a day's work for looking on the
work and deciding to do nothing. When the
masons were ready to build, the stones were
not ready for them to build with, or the mortar
was not mixed ; so they waited and talked,
and charged for having been on the spot with
nothing to do. When it came to plastering,
they were short of laths or short of nails, or
short of sand or short of lime—short of every-

thing except reasons for doing nothing. So
with the carpenters. They went to work to do
the thing the wrong way; and when it was
done, and they were convinced it was wrong,
they went to work and pulled it to pieces again;
and recommenced doing it in another way.
When the rain fell, or there was frost, masons,
plasterers, carpenters, plumbers, and painters
wanted to work outside, and saw clear reasons
why it was impossible to do anything inside;
and as the rain hindered or the frost prevented,
they went away with their hands in their
pockets and sat under a shed, looking at the
front of the house and the rain or the frost; and
charged for their desire to work when it was
not possible to work. When the sun shone
and the air was warm, they wanted to work indoors, and there were unanswerable reasons
why the work out of doors could not be got on
with. However, in spite of all these difficulties,
the house progressed, but progressed so slowly
as to astonish even the masons and carpenters
and plumbers and plasterers and painters themselves, and to comfort them greatly. They
were not going to kill the goose off-hand that
laid the golden egg, but pick him to pieces
feather by feather.

The plumbers laid the lead, and the masons
walked over it with hobnailed shoes, making

holes in it, which required a revision and a patching with solder of the lead which was quite new; and when the glass was put into the windows, the carpenters drove planks through the panes, necessitating new glazing. And the ironmonger brought grates that would not fit the chimney-pieces, and invoked the masons to pull out the mantel-pieces again and put them in afresh. Then he made holes in the plaster for the bell-wires so ragged and so big that the plasterers must needs come and mend them up again. Lastly, the glazier put his hand into putty or white paint and smeared a circle in the midst of every pane, to give work to a woman to clean the windows.

The painter performed wonders; he coloured all the wood-work of the house flesh-colour, and called that priming. Why it should be primed flesh-colour, he did not say. I remember how that there stood over the market hall in Launceston—and it stands there still—a clock on which are two figures with hammers, that strike the hours and the quarters. Many years ago, the civic authorities ordered the repainting of these automata. Then a painter went up on a scaffold and primed them, after the manner of painters, flesh-colour. The mayor issuing from the Guild Hall saw this, and was frightened, or shocked, and with mayoral mantle and gold chain of office about his shoulders, ran up the ladder and said : 'What are you about? We don't want to have Adam and Eve here.'

'I'm priming, your Worship,' answered the painter, 'as you were primed afore you drew on your clothes and insignia.'

Now, it is reasonable enough that figures representing human beings should be coloured pink first, and painted with clothing to taste, afterwards ; but why windows? Why doors? Why skirting-boards?

A recent writer on Natural Law and the Moral Order holds up to scorn the hermit lobster, which does not build its own shell, but seeks a ready-built house into which to slip. The writer of that book never had to do with the erection of a manse for himself, I presume, or he would have taken off his hat and bowed to the hermit lobster, and pointed him out as an example of instinct so acute that it reached wisdom.

Richard Cable had accepted the builder's rough estimate of cost and of time the house would take in building, and had left a margin ; but soon found that the margin should have been as wide as that in an *édition de luxe* book or of a modern funeral card. A builder can always discover reasons for spinning out the time, and especially the expense. Cable found, before the house was done, that he had spent all the money put by for it, and was obliged to borrow for its completion and for the furnishing; and this did not improve his humour. He had not allowed the house to be built by contract, because he knew very well that what is built by contract is badly built; and that if he were to pay an overlooker to see to his interests, the masons and the carpenters, and the plumbers and glaziers, and slaters and painters, would give the man an acknowledgment to overlook their bad work. So he had his house built by day-work, and then it was to the interest of the men to do their work in the most substantial and thorough manner, because that is also the most slow and costly manner.

When Cable was on his way back from each journey, he thought within himself: 'Now I shall see a great advance in the work; I have been away three weeks.' But on his arrival he required good-nature and faith to see that a proper amount of work had been done; and good-nature and faith fail when disappointed repeatedly. However, the house was finished at length and furnished—furnished quietly and scantily, because the money ran short. Richard was not alarmed. He knew

he would earn the necessary sum, but he was
sore at having to borrow. The consciousness
of being in debt was new to him, and fretted
his already sore spirit. It took the zest off the
pleasure of having a grand new house of his
own. He had no difficulty in getting the
money advanced by the bank; he was pretty
well known to be a man who made gold by
turning it about in his hands. It flattered his
pride to be able to borrow so easily, and yet it
galled him to know that the house was not
absolutely his own till the debt was cleared
away.

The house was finished; and it had seven
red windows in the upper storey, and three on
each side of the door below. To the door led
a flight of slate steps, and the door opened into
a spacious hall. The house looked larger than
it really was, because it was shallow. The hill
rose too rapidly in the rear to allow of much
back premises. In the garden was a summer-
house, as he had seen in his dream, painted
green, with a gilt knob at the top, very fresh
and shining.

When the house was complete, and ready
for him, he arrived from Somersetshire; and in
the evening, when the children were in bed,
his mother put the key on the table. 'There!'
said she. To-morrow we leave this old cottage

for the new house. Richard, why not take possession of it with a new heart? You are in the wrong now. She has been here many months, and all speak well of her. She works for her living, and works hard. There are no pride and stubbornness left in her; all that has passed from her into you; and the gentleness and pity and meekness are gone from you into her.'

He moved impatiently. He took up the key and threw it down; then he pushed it from one side of the table to the other, and his face was sullen. 'Mother,' he said, 'I would not allow another to speak to me of her. It is enough. You have said your say. I have suffered too much from her. I have said it. We are parted for ever.'

'You have not seen her.'

'I do not choose to see her.'

'But you should. She is greatly changed, and looks weak and frail. You do not think that the great alteration in her mode of life must hurt her. She is like a flower taken out of a garden and put on the moor, where every wind blows her about, and every animal that goes by tramples on her.'

'Who has dared to touch her?' asked Cable, flaring up.

'I do not mean that any one has purposely

wronged her ; but she is in a place and among people who do not understand her, and she cannot endure rough handling.  She is too delicate, and it will kill her.'

'What do you want, then ?  If I give her money, she will not take it.'

'Not if it be given churlishly.'

'Churlishly !  Are you also turned against me ? '

'You are acting wrongly.  I would not say so to another ; I would not let her suppose that I reproached you ; but in my heart I think it. I also went on for years harbouring my wrong, and believing that I could never forgive it ; but the time came when I was forced to forgive ; and you, Richard, you also must do the same.'

'You have said this before.  I cannot listen. I shall go away again ; ' and he put his hat on his head and went forth.

Next day, the few things required to be removed from the cottage were carted to the new house ; but Richard would not move into it till evening, when no one would be about to observe the migration.

The sun had set when they all started for Red Windows, the father leading, then Mrs. Cable and little Bessie, and the rest two and two, the twins of course together.  The youngest carried their toys, a battered doll, a

wooden horse; and the elder, sundry treasures
that could not be intrusted to other hands to
transport. The evening was still, soft, and
summery; bats flew about and screamed ear-
piercingly. The hedges were full of foxgloves
and wreathed with honeysuckle. Glowworms
shone in the banks, jewelling the way, as pixy
lamp-bearers welcoming them to their new
home. The procession moved slowly, because
Bessie was heavy to carry, and because Susie
could not walk fast. It moved silently, because
the children were depressed in spirits, sorry to
leave their little rooms and garden—the known
for the new, the loved for strange.

Cable spoke; but his voice startled him and
the rest. He felt not as if he were being advanced in position, but as if he were going to
execution. He turned and looked at his
mother. 'Let me carry Bessie now,' he said.
'What are you whispering?'

'I was not whispering.'

'I saw your lips moving.'

'I was repeating to myself some words
that kept coming up in my mind, like a cork
in water.'

'What words?'

'Merely a text, and I cannot say why they
rise.'

'What is the text?'

' " He shall lay the foundation in his first-born, and in his youngest shall he set up the gates." '

' What do you mean by that? '

' I mean nothing; but I cannot get the text out of my head. It seems to point——'

Cable laughed. ' This is mere superstition, mother. You have Cornish blood in you. Besides, the foundations are laid and the gates set up, and nothing has occurred.'

She said no more, nor did he; but the words she had spoken did not help to cheer him. Presently he found his own lips moving; he was repeating the ominous words; and a fear fell on him lest they might apply not to the bare walls and wooden gates, but to the domestic life in the new mansion—a new life to be built up amid new surroundings and in a new sphere. For, indeed, Richard by this move mounted the social scale. In the cottage, he was but a cottager; in the grand new house, he was transferred to the middle class. As Josephine went down, he went up.

He opened the garden gates, and the feet of the little procession trod the newly gravelled path. There were flower-beds, but no flowers; a lawn, but the grass was battered and cut up with the traffic of the builders. They came to the flight of steps, and Cable went up, put the key in the door, and tried to open it; but the wood was swollen, and the door stuck. He put his knee to it and forced it open, and the noise reverberated through the empty house like thunder. Then the children came in. The air within smelt of lime and paint. He struck a match and lighted a paraffin lamp. The children looked round in astonishment, but expressed no pleasure; they shivered; the night air had been cold, but the interior of this new house seemed colder still.

In the dining-room, a cold supper was laid— lamb and salad, whortleberry tart, and cream, blancmange—'Shaky trade, that is bluemange,' the woman called it who had cooked the supper, an old cook from the parsonage, married in the place.

'Sit down,' said Richard. 'Eat heartily your first meal in Red Windows.'

But the children were not hungry; his mother did not care to eat, and he himself had no appetite. He forced himself to take lamb, but he could hardly swallow it. The children were silent, looking about them at the walls and ceiling, and chimney-piece with the mirror over it.

'Well,' said Cable, 'as no one seems hungry, the sooner to bed the better.'

So they parted for the night.

Next morning, he was in his garden. The blacksmith appeared at the gate.

'Neighbour,' said he, 'glad to see you well quartered. I'm sorry I haven't been over the house; the iron work was not given to me, but to a Camelford man. I'd have served you better. However, I bear no malice. I should like to see over the box, if you've no objections.'

'Box! What box? Do you call a mansion with seven windows on the front in the upper storey and six below—a box? I have objections to show my box, as you call it.'

'Oh, I meant no offence,' said Penrose. 'I'll come another day.'

'This is not a showplace,' said Cable curtly.

The next to come was the innkeeper. 'Halloh! Mr. Cable! Shake hands. Glad to see you. We've lost our guardian—died the other day; so we've had a vestry meeting and elected you guardian of the poor, unanimous.'

'I—guardian of the poor! the poor of St. Kerian?' He laughed bitterly. 'No one cared for me and watched over me when I was poor and ill. Why should I care for your poor and be their guardian, now I am rich?'

'Come, Cable, don't be sour. Give a sovereign, and we'll have the bells rung for your house-warming.'

'Not one penny. It concerns no one but

myself and my family that I enter Red Windows.'

The taverner shook his head and went away. Then his mother came to him and said: 'Richard, why do you not meet the St. Kerian people in a friendly way, when they make the first step towards good-fellowship? Why do you refuse the hand that is held out for yours? Why should you be angered that they look on you now with other eyes than those with which they saw you enter the parish? When you broke stones on the road, what was there in you to attract their esteem? When they saw your love and care for your children, they respected you; and when they found you were making money, they acknowledged that you had brains. Was not that natural and reasonable and right? When you were poor, with seven hungry mouths crying for food, there were others worse off than yourself, and what sympathy did you show them? When a crippled beggar came through the village, did you rush after him, take off your hat, and offer him hospitality? Why, then, are you angry with the St. Kerian people because they only begin to touch their hats and notice you, now that you are well off? You are well off because you have talents above their level, and this they recognise.'

'I wonder what *she* thinks, now that we are in our house, when she sees the smoke rising from the chimneys, and the windows lighted up?'

'She thinks that a cottage where love is, is better than a thirteen-windowed mansion where there is hardness of heart and pride.'

Richard did not answer; he walked away, and went about his grounds and planned improvements, and seated himself in his garden-house, and tried to believe he was happy. At night, when alone, he sat again in his summer-house with the door open, and looked down at St. Kerian, which lay in the valley, with a gossamer veil hanging over it, the vapour in the air condensing above the stream. The church tower stood out like ivory against the black yews. He could see the chimneys of the parsonage, and the glitter of the tiny conservatory flashing the moonbeams back. He heard the soothing rush of the water in the mill 'leat' running the waste water into the river. In the wood behind, the owls were hooting. On such a night as this he had stood at his cottage window there below, two years ago, and resolved to realise his dream. He had accomplished what he had determined, and was he satisfied? He strained his eyes to see the old cottage; but it was dark; but, through the soft haze, he saw one golden pin-point, from where the post-office stood. Was that *her* light? Was she sitting there, at the window, looking up, out of the valley, at his grand house, on which the moonlight shone? What were her thoughts?

Richard Cable's breast heaved, and a choke came in his breath. He turned his face away and looked at the hills, at the gray moor frosted with moonlight, at the deep sky, and tried to spell stars in it, but could not, because of the suffused light. Then his eyes went back to the golden speck, the one spangle of yellow in the cold scene of white and gray and black. Then he stood up, and sat with his back to the door, and looked into the gloom of the interior, and down at the rectangular oblong patch of white, like snow on the floor, laid there by the moon. But he could not long study that. He turned on his seat, and once again the golden speck shot into his brain and down into his heart, where it fell like a spark and burnt him, that he uttered a suppressed cry.

'It is all stubbornness and pride,' he said, rubbing the bench with his hand, as if to polish it. 'She is determined to show me that she can do without me. What does my mother mean by saying the rough life is killing her? She has chosen it out of obstinacy, to spite me.

If I were to give her five pounds a week, she would throw them down at my feet. I can do nothing. If she is determined to kill herself, she must do so. She is proud. Why is her light burning now? She is working on late, that she may earn money and do without help. It is flint and steel striking, and the spark— there it is, and it is burning me.'

## CHAPTER LIV.

### 'NO FOOL LIKE AN OLD FOOL.'

'I SUPPOSE,' said Richard Cable to his mother, 'that *she* would not live in our cottage? Not if I offered it her rent free?'

'The cottage is mine, Richard, not yours. Perhaps from me she would take it, but not from you.'

'Then you may offer it her.' He had his hands in his pockets; he drew them sharply forth and began to hum a tune — it was the Mermaid's song from *Oberon*. When he thought of her, that tune came up with the thought. 'Mother,' he said, breaking off in the midst of the tune, 'now that we are in this house, we are in a different position, and the little girls must be suited to it. I've heard them talking just like the St. Kerian children —with a Cornish twang, and I won't have it. They must have better schooling than they can get at the national school.'

'Will you send them away?' asked Mrs.

Cable in dismay, as her heart failed her at the
thought of parting with her grandchildren.

'No ; they must not leave home ; they must
learn better here. They should be able to play
on the piano, and to sing, and read French, and
know something of all those concerns which
young ladies are expected to be acquainted
with.'

'What! Are you going to bring a gover-
ness into the house to them ?' asked Mrs. Cable
with dismay almost equal to the first at the
prospect of parting with the children.

'No ; I'll have no stranger here,' he
answered.

'Then, how are they to learn ?'

'Is there no one in the village who could
teach them ? I do not mean that they should
be ignorant, or know no more than the
labourers' children, because they will have
money, and if they marry, they shall marry
well.'

'There is a long time to that,' said Mrs.
Cable.

'Who can teach them ?' asked Richard.

'There is but one person who can do this,'
answered she, after a pause.

'She must be well paid for her trouble.
You must arrange all that. Only, I will not
have this teacher come here ; the children must

go to her. Pay her what you like, and take her, whoever she may be. I do not ask her name; I want to know nothing about her; but if she teaches them, I will not have her too free with them: she must undertake not to kiss them, and coax them to love her. Do not tell me who she is; I do not want to know. I leave all that to you, but I make my stipulations beforehand.'

'You mean this, Richard?'

'I leave it to you. I ask no questions. I want no names named. If the children are to learn the piano, this lady who is to teach them must have one on which they may be taught. I will order one at Launceston to be sent to the cottage.'

'Very well, Richard.'

'I have hit on a great idea,' said he with a sudden change of tone. 'There is always a trouble about feeding the calves with the hand. I have ordered at Bridgewater a lot of stone bottles, like those for ginger-beer, but as large as foot-warmers for bed. And I've had a board put along each side of the calves' van, with holes in it, into which the bottles can be fitted. And then, mother, I've had tubes and nipples made for the bottles; and I pass these into the calves through the bars, and they can all suck comfortably as they ride along. I might take a patent for it, I fancy, if I chose.'

'But, Richard, to go back to the subject——'

He interrupted her hastily. 'I'm going to engage a boy; and when we come to a hill, he'll walk round the van, and if any of the calves, which are as weak in their intellects as babies, let the nipples out of their mouths, which they may do through the joggling of the van when the roads are fresh stoned, or they may do it out of sheer stupidity—then, I say, the boy will put them back in their mouths again, and fill up the bottles with skim-milk at our halting-places. I've always found the calves get very much pulled down by a journey, and now, with this contrivance, I reckon they will be very much pulled up.'

'But about the girls?'

'I'm going to work on a grander scale altogether, and have a set of vans. I'm quite sure I can carry on the business wholesale, and with this idea of the calves' sucking-bottles carried out into execution, I must succeed.'

There was no getting anything more out of him relative to the education of the children. He was apparently now engrossed in the perfecting of his arrangements for feeding the calves out of bottles.

'It is wearing and exhausting to the hand,' he said. 'It gets like that of a washerwoman who uses soda—all cockled and soft, what with being in the milk and in the calves' mouths. I've tried the butt-end of the driving-whip, but it don't draw up milk, and the calves don't like the taste of the brass mount; so I've had to come back to the hand again. It is possible they may object to the vulcanised india-rubber at first, whilst it is fresh.' Then, abruptly he reverted to what he had spoken of before. 'Don't let *her* think that there's any favour shown in letting her have the cottage. It is done to suit my convenience. Last night, as I sat in my summer - house, I could see down into the village, and, I suppose to annoy me, she had her lamp burning till late, and there is not a wall or a tree between the post-office and my garden, so that the light of her lamp shone right up in at my door, and sit how I would, I could not get away from it. It aggravated me, and I know I shall get no pleasure out of my summer-house like that. By day, she'll do something to annoy me if she has that window —perhaps put red geraniums in it.'

'But, Richard—it is a mile away.'

'I don't know what the distance is; it aggravates and provokes me past endurance. I shan't be able to sit there of a day, because of

the pelargoniums ; nor at night, because of her
lamp. I shall have to move the summer-house,
and the expense and trouble of that—the having
masons and carpenters and painters about the
place again, will be so vexing, that I'd rather
she went into our old cottage. It would be
best for me, and she'd save money herself, for
I don't mind the rent, as it is an accommodation to me. I couldn't move the summer-house
under ten pounds.'

'And with regard to the matter of the
children——'

'There is no favour there, either,' interrupted Richard ; 'and I beg you will let her
understand that. I want them instructed, and
there is no one here but the young ladies at the
parsonage and herself fit to teach them ; and
you can ask the former to undertake the task ;
if they refuse, then you can offer it to the other
one ; she gets the job only because there is no
one else available. Let her understand that.
And mind, tell her, if I send a piano there--I
mean to the cottage—it is not that I give it her
or lend it her : it is for my daughters to practise on ; but I don't object to her playing on it
at any other time, because I've always heard
that a piano ought to be played on continually
to keep it in tune. It would go badly out
of tune if it were only used for the children's

schooling, and that would spoil their ear.—
Also,' continued Cable, 'there are some sticks
of furniture, and some bedding and other stuff,
and some crockery down there, which must be
used to keep the damp out of them, and the
moth and the wood-worm. There's no room
up here for all these things, and they don't
suit this new house; they are left down there
to accommodate me; and if she does not pay
rent, it is because we find it convenient to put
someone in to keep the cottage dry, the mildew
out of the furniture, and the moths from the
bedding, and to keep the crockery from being
chipped. Make her understand that; and if
she spoils things, she'll have to pay damages.
I do not know that I shan't put some more
things into the cottage just to run the chance
of their being injured by her, and so deduct
the cost of the things spoiled from her wages.'
Then, without looking at his mother to see
what she thought of his ideas, whether relating
to the feeding-bottles for his calves, or the
education of his children, he went down into
the valley to his old cob cottage.

He had put the key in a secret place—a
hole in the thatch, that none but he knew of.
He opened the door and went in and locked
himself in. The cottage was in the same condition in which it had been left. The stools

were round the poor little table, the armchair
by the fire, and the ashes of the peat white on
the hearth. Then he took off his coat, and
went into the back kitchen and fetched a
broom and a pail and a pan, and set to work
to clean the house. He did not return to Red
Windows all day. He was busy at the cottage.
He scrubbed the floors and the little stairs ; he
brushed down the walls ; then he got whiting
at the grocer's and whitewashed ceiling and
walls. He cleaned up the hearth, and laid
fresh kindling-wood on it, and hung a kettle to
the crook over it. He paid repeated visits to
the shop that day, and bought glazed calico and
tacks, and chintz and muslin ; and he nailed
up curtains to the windows, and put blinds
where there were none—' lest,' as he said to
himself, ' the lamp should shine out of those
windows and torment me.' Afterwards, he got
a spade and dug up and tidied the garden. He
did not desist from his self-imposed task till late
at night, not till everything was done to his
satisfaction. He was a man who loved tidiness.
Next morning early, he left St. Kerian. This
time he went to Bewdley, where he had to
bestow some cattle he had contracted to bring
to the farmer on the home-farm of the manor.

When he came to the inn, he found Mr.
Polkinghorn there, who sprang up, and saluted

him with urbanity. 'How are we?' asked the footman; 'bobbish or not? And how is the missus?'

'I am well,' answered Cable gravely. He passed over the second query.

'You haven't come in your travels yet on the manor of Polkinghorn, have you?' inquired the flunky. 'Because, if we could hit on that, there'd be some chance of our recovering the title-deeds, and being reinstalled in our manorial rights. But—you see—till we know where it is, the Polkinghorns can take no step.'

'How go matters with you?' asked Cable.

'Well, queerish,' answered the footman. 'You've heard the news, of course?'

'News? I've heard nothing.'

'Not of our appointment to a bishopric?'

'You. No, certainly.'

'Yes, we are.'

'What? The old lady?'

'Not exactly; but her brother-in-law, old Sellwood. I know him well; he's a nice old shaver. He's going to be a bishop down your way, at Bodmin. That is in Cornwall, is it not?'

'Yes. *He* to be bishop! I do not look at the papers.'

'Yes; he'll be bishop. I don't know that

we care much about it. You see the families
of Sellwood and Otterbourne don't need it.
They've lots of money, and a twopenny-ha'-
penny bishopric ain't much to them ; especially
a new affair, such as this. Why, I don't believe there's even a cathedral there, not a dean
and chapter ; and—I wouldn't take a bishopric
myself where there wasn't a dean and chapter
to sit upon. If you don't sit upon somebody,
you're nobody. It isn't a man's headpiece that
gives him estimation ; it is his capacity elsewhere for sitting upon people. What is it that
makes Mr. Vickary so much respected in our
place ? It is that he sits upon us all. If he
only sat on the button-boy, would he be held
in such high honour ? I put it to you, as a
man of the world.'

Cable made no reply.

' I think if I may volunteer a suggestion,'
said Polkinghorn, ' that I could give you one
to improve your business.'

' Indeed ? '

' I suppose you've curates down your way ? '

' O yes, there are some.'

' When the bishop comes into quarters,
there will be a demand for more—for lots.'

' You think so ? '

' I'm sure of it,' said the flunky. ' Now,
add to your van of calves another of curates,

and dispose of them down in Cornwall.—
You'll excuse me; I am accounted a joker.'
Then looking round, and seeing that Mrs.
Stokes was not in the room, he said in a low
tone : 'There is worse behind. We're about
to have a regular revolution.'

'Of what sort?'

'You'd never guess; and you're somehow
mixed up in it.'

'How is that?'

'About that affair of—your wife.'

'What about her?' sharply.

'It seems she has a stylish sort of a father,
called Cornellis.'

'Yes, what then?'

'He came here after you took her away.
He didn't appear whilst she was in our place.
He's a gentleman, you know, and I suppose
disapproved of her being in a situation;
though, for the matter of that, I'm a Polkinghorn, and I'm in a situation. What a
Polkinghorn can do, a Cable may.'

'Never mind about that; go on.'

'Some folks have vulgar objections to situa-
tions. If they do object to them, they're not
gentlemen; as I take it, it is low.'

'What has Mr. Cornellis done?'

'Done! You should ask, what is he going
to do?'

'Then I do ask that. He has not been to see his daughter where she is now.'

'Oh, I don't fancy he's particularly interested about her. I fancy she was made the excuse for his first coming here, and making our old girl's acquaintance. He's been here off and on a good deal since—a great deal too much for the liking of some of us; and if Miss Otterbourne had taken our opinion, she'd have sent him about his business long ago.—I beg pardon if I offend. He is your father-in-law.'

'You do not offend at all.'

'It was a bit of a come-down his girl marrying you, no doubt, and he cut her off and disowned her for it; but he seemed mighty interested about her after she was gone.'

'He had not sufficient interest to pursue her, and see that she was well and comfortable and in good hands.'

'In good hands! She was in yours, I suppose, comfortable! It seems to me you're not badly off. Besides, as you married her, she was your charge, not his.'

'What further has Mr. Cornellis done?'

'He has made himself a great favourite with the old lady; he humours her, and—— But here comes Mrs. Stokes, and I don't like to talk state secrets before her. I'll tell you later.

We were speaking of the bishop. Do you know Sellwood?'

'I have spoken to our rector at Hanford.'

'I can't say I'm intimate with him,' said Mr. Polkinghorn. 'There are some people one can't be intimate with; though one may put out as many feelers as an octopus, there is no laying hold of them. I've taken his shaving-water to him, too.'

This did not seem to interest Cable; he was anxious to hear the rest about Josephine's father. Presently, Mrs. Stokes left the room, and then Mr. Polkinghorn resumed the subject.

'He's an insinuating man is your father-in-law; and when he found that the old woman was keen on the lost Tribes, bless you, he led her such a tally-ho! after them, it was just like as you play with a kitten, drawing a ball, or a cork along the floor, and whisk and away went the old creature purring and frisking and snapping and clawing. It was quite pretty to see her. And I do believe that he persuaded her that he was the concentration of the Ten Tribes in himself, a sort of a mixed pickle-bottle of capsicum and gherkin, and cauliflower and onion—only put Benjamin and Manasses, and Gad and the rest of 'em, for the vegetables, and a general Judaic flavour for the vinegar.'

'Go on. What next?'

'I should like to know what are the circumstances of your father-in-law? Is he a
man of substance or a soap-bubble—which?'

'I cannot say; I suspect the latter.'

'So do I; and I fancy he will take care to
make himself a comfortable nest somewhere.
There was a goose and a gander on intimate
terms, that I knew, and the latter set to ripping
the down off the breast of the goose to line a
nest. He persuaded her to it, and the fond
creature helped to strip her own breast; and
the two birds smoothed the down into a very
snug sort of nest. Well, will you believe me?
—there came a late fall of snow and some very
sharp weather, and through it all, the gander
sat in the downy nest, and let the goose walk
about and shiver in the snow, with her plucked
breast quite bare.'

'What do you mean by this?'

'Oh, I'm a wag, and I mean more than I
put in plain words. There are parables to be
read, and the moral is easy understood by
them as has brains. I don't feel sure that
your father-in-law has not the nature of that
gander, and I'm pretty sure our old woman
has that of the goose that helped to pluck
herself.'

'Do you mean to say that he is helping himself to her money?'

'I won't say that. But I believe before
long he'll persuade her to pay for a marriage
license, and then he'll take up his quarters in
Bewdley and begin the plucking process. We
won't stand it—none of us. We will go.'

'But—she is old enough to be his mother.'

'There is no fool like an old fool.'

## CHAPTER LV.

### TO THE GALLOPERS.

CAPTAIN EDWARD G., my paternal great-great-uncle, was a notable horseman in his day. Astley, the founder of the equestrian theatre that was the delight of boys in my youth, but which has passed away with Sadler's Wells, Vauxhall, and the Colosseum, Regent's Park, was in his troop, and from him acquired his skill in horsemanship. Among Captain Edward's feats was one in which the pupil never equalled his master. He threw down the several gold links of a chain at irregular intervals along a high-road, and then, striking spurs into his horse, galloped over the course, and as he came to a link, swung himself down, picked it off the ground, recovered his position in the saddle, and so along the whole road, till he had collected in his left hand without exception all the scattered links.

The modern novel-reader emulates the achievements of Captain G., and the novel-writer is expected to distribute the several links of connection of his story along the ground at such regular intervals and in such conspicuous places as shall facilitate the reader's picking them up. The author must, moreover, well water and roll the way, and make it very straight, and be content if the gallopers over his course succeed in picking up some, though not all, of his story-links. The reader is essentially a Galloper. He, or more generally, she, goes at the novel with dug-in spur and slashing whip and jerk of rein. The words are flown over as blades of grass, the chapter heads are passed as telegraph poles; away goes the galloper through page after page, faster, ever faster; there is no time for breathing or looking about; the descriptions are splashed through, the conversations skimmed, the moralisings skipped, the less important incidents are jumped; nothing is considered but how to reach the end as fast as possible, with a fair sample of links in the hand.

Now, consider! The writer has to write for these Gallopers. Is not the thought sufficient to take all heart out of him? An experienced writer who for a lifetime has catered for the reading public, and knows their proclivities as Sir John Lubbock knows earthworms, and Miss Ormerod knows blight, said to me : ' You will never become a popular novelist until you alter your style. You set before the novel-reader moral problems hard to unravel, and make your terminations sad. The novel-reader wants *neither to be made to think nor to be made to feel.*' In a word, I must lay myself out for the Gallopers. Lay myself out for the Gallopers ! Is there a form of degradation deeper to which a literary man can descend? I must let myself be watered and rolled as a tennis-ground, to be raced over by the hundred thousand with voided brains, vapid hearts, mule-witted, caprice-led, the purposeless, pulse-less, nerveless, characterless, without a noble aim or a high ambition, without having felt the needle-point, and had an arc begun about their sheep-heads of the golden nimbus of self-abnegation.

No ; I will not lay myself out to be trampled by the idle feet of the ignoble herd of Gallopers. Let them turn aside when they note my ruggedness. I will throw up ridges and sink pitfalls, and be humpy and lumpy. Let them take the profanation of their tread off earnest work.

It is not the thoughtful and those with pur-suits in life who are the novel-readers ; it is the vast multitude of the do-nothing, whose whole aim is distraction, who read to kill thought, to kill

healthy feeling, serious purpose, good resolution,
generous impulse—to kill God's precious gift of
Time.    Shall I lay myself out for such as they ?
I can understand Faust selling his soul to the
devil for youth ;  or the architect of Cologne
Minster for fame,  or many another for wealth.
But there is an infamy worse than that, and
that is the sale to the Galloping novel-reader.
Asmodeus,  Mephistopheles,  Satan,  call  him
what  you  will,  is  an  *Intelligence*;  but  the
modern novel-reader,  Gwendoline or Edith,  or
Mabel or Florence,  whatever her name be, is a
soap-bubble,  void of everything but an evan-
escent exterior in iridescence.    Lay myself out
as  a  rolling-ground  for  these  bubbles,  blown
along by the wind !    God forbid !    I would tear
myself  to  pieces  with  my  own  hands  rather
than stoop to such baseness.

So—if  I  choose  to  force  uncomfortable
thoughts on  my readers' minds—I will.    If I
choose to end my story unhappily—I will.    I
consider my  own  standards,  and  measure  my
work by them.

In the ' Compère Mathieu,' a French story
of last century,  the penultimate chapter shows
us the hero in prison,  brought there by a logical
sequence of events,  chained hand and foot, with
the gallows  preparing  for him  outside  the jail.
In the final chapter we are abruptly introduced

to the compère at large, opulent, esteemed, and wealthy. The reader asks naturally, ' But how has this sudden transformation come about?' The author answers : ' I know no more than do you. My publisher told me that readers desire a novel to end happily, so I have ended mine happily. If the termination does not fit on to the events that go before, that is your affair, not mine.'

I will not say that my publishers and my readers are so exacting as to force me to do this ; but they hit me very hard on another point. Both insist on a story being three volumes in length, or sixty chapters. Now, when Richardson wrote, he was allowed to occupy seven volumes with the affairs of Sir Charles Grandison, and of Clarissa Harlowe, and so leisurely to unfold his story and develop his characters. We authors now have not this liberty, and we are forced to crush our story into less than half that length. To do this, we are obliged to do our work imperfectly ; we cannot follow the thread of the story evenly to the end, and show every stage in the history of our heroes and heroines. As characters are moulded and grow, we want time and leisure to exhibit the growth and indicate the process of modelling ; but we have our hands tied by the inexorable system of three volumes. My readers—I am not addressing the Gallopers, whom I have scared away, and who are careering wildly, purposelessly elsewhere, kicking up their heels at me, as the ass at the sick lion—my readers—my few left, who are also my special friends—must excuse me if I am forced to carry them hastily over a twelvemonth, and to put into their hands some of the links of the chain, without many words.

Mr. Sellwood has been consecrated Bishop of Bodmin; and Mr. Cornellis has married the old lady, Miss Otterbourne, and is engaged plucking his goose, and lining his nest with her feathers. Mary Cable is growing up into a tall, beautiful girl, with eyes so blue and full of sun that when she looks into the face of a man, he is dazzled, as if looking into the summer sky. The children are all grown, and they are all, moreover, vastly improved by the teaching they have received at the cottage from Josephine. But as to any approximation between their father and Josephine, there was none apparent; in that particular all was where it was.

Mary was the pride and joy of her father's heart. He loved all his children, but he was most proud of Mary, and justly; her equal was not to be found thereabouts. That the young men looked after her and admired her, was right; it was her due, but, thought

Richard, she shall be given to none of them.
Not one of them deserves such a treasure.
Cable continued at his business. With seven
girls to provide for, he must make a good deal
of money, and all the money he made he put
away in the Duchy Bank, paying off in instal-
ments his debt on the house. His improved
position brought him more in contact with the
people of St. Kerian than before, when he was
a poor stone-breaker on the roadside. His
sourness disappeared, but in its place came
pride. He spoke with the farmers and trades-
men, and they respected him, his talents, his
practical good sense; but the barrier between
them was not wholly broken down. He had
no intention that it should be. Towards his
own children, he had always been kind, and
indeed indulgent; but the change in his temper,
his hardness, sternness, bitterness towards
those without, had gradually and imperceptibly
affected his conduct towards his own within his
household. He was kind, indeed, and indulgent
still; but he lacked now what he had possessed
of old, when he had had a childlike spirit, that
perception of the requirements of joyous children's souls, full of exuberant life, which is that
which endears elders to their children. If he
would have made his daughters happy in his
society, he should have sought happiness in

himself, laid up there a store of it, from which to distribute to all who sought it at his hands. But instead, in the granary of his heart was a harvest of much ill-seed.

One day, Mrs. Cable said to him when he was alone: 'I don't know what you think about it, Richard, but it is right that you should know that young Walter Penrose is mightily taken up with Mary. He's a fine fellow, and nobody can say a bad word of him. He has been some few years in Launceston, and now he is home again, and is likely to follow in his father's shop, after the old blacksmith gives up. As children, they have always had a liking to each other, and now he is here, I see he is after Mary. In church it seems as though he could not keep his eyes off her; and whenever she goes into the village he is sure to be in front of the blacksmith's shop to have a talk with her. She is very young yet, only seventeen; but—she must marry some day; and if you see no reasons against it, they might come to an understanding, and wait a twelvemonth.'

Then Cable's wrath foamed up. 'I do see reasons against it,' he said. 'I see what this means. Because I have worked and made money, and the St. Kerian people can't break into the bank and rob me of my money there, they set their sons on to follow my girls. I suppose the saddler's son, and the cobbler's boy, and the miller's, and the chimney sweep's, if there were one, would all be looking for a seventh of my earnings, by snapping up one of my daughters, and so I should have moiled and toiled for St. Kerian folk, that they might spend.'

'But if the girls should like the lads. There is nothing against Walter Penrose; and I believe that Mary——'

'It is enough that I will not have it,' said Cable impatiently. 'She likes what I like, and has no desire beyond my will.'

One Sunday afternoon, after church service, old Penrose the blacksmith came out through the graveyard alongside of Cable. The girls walked behind, Mary with Martha; then the twins Effie and Jane, who were inseparable; and then the rest. The blacksmith was a fine man, broad-shouldered, big-handed, with very black eyes, but soft as velvet, and black hair the colour of the culm in his smithy —now, however, dusted with gray, as though ash had got among it. Instead of turning away at the gate to go to his home, he walked on with Cable. He did not live adjoining his smithy. The shop was on the road to Red Windows. Penrose talked a good deal; Cable answered, but was not a great speaker. All

the better company—he was a good listener.
Penrose talked about this and about that, and
Cable nodded. He was wondering why the
blacksmith accompanied him beyond his own
house.

Presently Penrose said : 'Well, Mr. Cable,
I reckon we're getting on in life, and want to
see the young people settled. I know my
missus be mad set on it, and I should be glad
to have my son fixed here. He knows his
trade, and there's plenty of work to keep both
him and me.'

Cable jerked his head impatiently.

'My Walter is a proper lad ; though I'm
his father, I say it. You may look round St.
Kerian and you'll hardly find a better ; and
the maiden he fancies——'

Then Cable stood still and turned, and
looked down the road ; he saw the little group
that followed had been invaded. Young Walter
Penrose was there, between Martha and Mary ;
but his eyes and his words were directed only
to Mary. All the blood in Cable's body
spurted to his face, and his eyes glared like the
blacksmith's forge when the bellows were in
full blast. 'What do you mean ?' he asked
hoarsely.

'I mean this,' answered Penrose, 'that my
Walter has set his heart on your Mary, and I

reckon the maiden is not contrary. I'm agreeable.'

The colour went out of Cable's face; his lips assumed a livid and bitter appearance. 'Indeed,' he said, 'you are agreeable, are you? *I'm not.*' He turned; he had reached the gate to his garden; and he beckoned the girls to come on. He saw the blacksmith shake his head as he met his son; then he saw the colour disappear from Mary's cheek, and when she came to the gate her head was drooping, and, if he could have seen her eyes, he would have seen them full of tears.

After that, it seemed as though a bar of ice had formed between him and his eldest daughter—a bar which no sunray of love could melt. The gentle Mary said not a word. She was meek, obedient, docile as ever; but she did not meet her father's eye with her former frank smile, nor seek his society unsolicited.

Martha became petulant, pouted, and seemed to harbour a wrong, and resent it. Effie and Jane, the twins, looked on him with shyness, and when he came upon them laughing and talking, they became silent, and answered his questions with manifest timidity. Had his children ceased to love him? No; but they had begun to think of him as one who might stand between them and perfect happi-

ness, one who might spoil their brightest
schemes.

Cable became more morose. He watched
Mary. He saw that she was unhappy ; that
she was becoming pale and thin ; the joy of
her life seemed withered, her eyes had lost
their sparkle, and the dimple rarely formed
now about her lips. 'I see what it is,' said
Cable to himself. 'She will not forget that
young Penrose, till she has found some one
else to regard. I'll talk to Jacob Corye.' So
he rode over to the 'Magpie' at Pentargon.

Mr. Corye was a prosperous man. Cable,
who had had such close dealings with him,
knew that he had put by a good deal of money.
Moreover, Cable could not forget the debt he
owed to Corye for having put him on the road
to make his fortune. Corye owned a very
considerable farm, as well as the 'Magpie' inn.
Of late, he had purchased a second farm, and
helped by Cable, he was fast becoming the
most prosperous yeoman of his district. He
kept on the inn more out of habit than for
necessity. Shortly after this visit to the 'Magpie,' Jacob Corye and his son Joshua were
invited to supper at Red Windows, and then
Cable and his two elder daughters were invited
to spend an evening at Pentargon. Little
Bessie had been failing of late, complaining of

her back, looking pinched in face, white and frail.

'I have asked Mr. and Mrs. Corye,' said Richard Cable, 'to let Bessie go to them for a bit. Do you not think, mother, that the sea air may brace her up? You see here we have our backs to the winds that blow over the Atlantic; but at Pentargon she will draw them into her lungs, fresh off the water.'

'No doubt it will do her good,' answered Mrs. Cable. 'But who is to be there with her?'

'Mary or Martha.'

'But Mary or Martha cannot stay there long, and I think you should give Bessie six weeks, or, better, a couple of months by the sea, before the winter sets in.'

'Mary cannot remain at Pentargon above a fortnight.'

'Then,' said Mrs. Cable, and looked her son hard in the eyes, 'let *her* go with the child. She will care for her—as a mother; and it will do her good also. She is looking weak and frail, as if she were wasting away. Hope deferred maketh the heart sick, and the body breaks down under a sick heart.'

'Make what arrangements you will, but do not consult me,' said Richard. 'Jacob and I have a fine scheme on hand. It was his notion,

but he did not see his way to getting it
clearly worked out till I helped him.  It is to
build a large hotel on the cliffs, and to adver-
tise it well; and then there will be streams of
people come there all the summer and autumn
for the splendid air and scenery.  There is to
be a flight of steps cut in the rock down to the
bay, where there will then be a first-class
bathing-place.  Jacob will make many thousand pounds by the speculation, see if he does
not, and I shall venture my savings in the
same.  It is sure to answer.'

'You think of nothing save making money,'
sighed Mrs. Cable.

Now, occasionally, on Sundays, young
Joshua Corye came over to church at St.
Kerian, and walked back with the Cable girls
as far as the gate, when Richard asked him to
step in and have tea with the party before
riding home to the 'Magpie.'  Joshua came
over ostensibly to bring Richard tidings of his
little Bessie, who was at Pentargon, and to beg
she might stay on there.  The child was not
well, weak, but ceased to complain, and enjoyed the fresh air.  The young person who
was with her was most attentive and gentle
with the feeble child.

'I don't want to hear about her,' said
Cable.  'Tell me about Bessie; and what your

father has done further about the hotel. I've a notion, tell him, that it must be called "Hotel Champagne Air," because the air you breathe on those cliffs goes sparkling and effervescing down your throat into your lungs. And, I fancy, the name would draw.'

Young Joshua Corye was a steady, decent young man, with a very fresh-coloured round face and small brown eyes. So fresh-coloured were his cheeks that if they had been skinned, they could not have been redder. He was a dull young man ; he could talk of harriers and badger-hunting, and rat-catching and rabbit-shooting, and boating, but of nothing else. He always wore very tight half-trousers, half-breech, buttoned over the calf from the knee to the ankle.

Cable was very keen on the idea of the Champagne Air Hotel, and he had pitched on Joshua Corye for Mary, because he was quite sure the hotel would prove a vast success. Old Jacob would pocket a great deal of money, and the fortunes of the young people would be made. Of late, batches of knapsacked young men and gangs of athletic old maids had taken to walking along the north-west coast of Devon and Cornwall, and the accommodation was scant for visitors. Cable schemed a coach in connection with the Exeter and Launceston

coach, which would carry passengers right on
to Champagne Air Hotel. It might be made
a sanatorium, a great bathing establishment.
The possibilities of making money out of it
were numerous. Jacob Corye had his own
farms, and could supply his hotel from his
farms, and so create a market in his midst.

Now that Bessie was at the 'Magpie,'
Richard did not go over and see her; but he
was eager to hear tidings of her. Before she
went there, he frequently rode over; now, not
at all.

Cable was sitting in his summer-house one
warm day, when he observed young Walter
Penrose coming up the hill with some iron
staples he had been lengthening for a farmer
beyond Red Windows. At the same time,
Mary was coming down the road with a pitcher
for water to a spring where the water was
softer than that of the well, and better suited
for her flowers. Richard Cable watched them
with some curiosity. They were both unaware
that his eye was on them. They passed each
other very close to him. He could see Walter's
dark eyes full of entreaty, fixed on Mary, and
that he let fall some of the staples. Mary
hung her head; she did not speak, she did not
look at him; but she went on to the spring. A
moment after, when Walter had turned the

corner and was out of sight, Cable heard her sink upon the step of his summer-house and burst into sobs. She had laid her head against the doorpost with her hands over her eyes, and she wept there for a quarter of an hour; her father listening, agitated within, unwilling to come forth and reveal that he had witnessed her sorrow.

He was troubled for some days after that; he was half-tempted to relent, but his pride stood in the way. He would not go to old Penrose, cap in hand, and ask him to accept Mary as his daughter-in-law. Besides, he and old Corye had settled between them that Joshua and Mary were to be installed together in Champagne Air Hotel.

'Mother,' he said, 'there's going to be a confirmation in St. Kerian's Church, and the bishop—our old parson at Hanford—is coming. There is not one of my girls as yet confirmed; they shall be confirmed together, all seven.— Don't tell me that Mary is too old, nor Bessie too young. It is my wish. And, mind you send to that person who does the needlework, and tell her to get ready seven white dresses for the seven girls, before the bishop comes. I don't know, but perhaps he'll be pleased to confirm the seven little maids, all of whom he baptised at Hanford; and I'm not sure but I shall be pleased to see him—if he's not forgotten me.'

'Richard,' said Bessie Cable, 'there is a white silk dress that *she* wore at her wedding. She gave it to me to do what I wished with, to cut it up for the children if I liked. Shall I use that for one of them ? '

Then Richard Cable's face became red as blood.

'No! ' he said. 'Do not touch it. Seven white robes, and this—an eighth.'

# CHAPTER LVI.

## A LAST TRIAL.

JOSEPHINE sat on a bench behind the 'Magpie' with little Bessie in her arms, looking out seaward. There was a good deal of cloud in the sky, but torn, with intervals of sky, through which the sun poured a rain of white light over the water. Seen from the great height of the cliffs, the Atlantic looked like a silvery-gray quivering sheet of satin, with folds of gray, and flashes and flakes and furls of brilliant white. About the headland of Pentargon, or King Arthur's Head, the breakers tossed, and the water was converted into milk. In the bay, under the cliffs, the gulls were noisy, and their voices, in laughter or objurgation, were re-echoed by the black precipices, multiplied and magnified, till, looking on, one wondered that so much and such strange sound should come from the flying flakes of white that glanced here and there. The wind was from the west; it had not brushed land since it left Labrador;

but it had lost its chill and harshness in passing over these endless tracts of ocean ; though it blew so strongly that it lifted and would have carried away an unsecured hat, there was a warmth and mellowness in it that divested it of all severity. It was like the reproof of a mother, charged with love and working betterment.

The horizon was full of change and mystery, now dark as a mourning-ribbon, now clear and white as that of a bride ; now it was a broad belt, then a single thread ; now melting into the sky, then sharp against it. Far away, it was blotted out by a blur of falling rain, or shadow from a cloud ; and here again by a veil of sunlight that was let down between the clouds, hiding all behind.

The air was full of music—the roar of the sea, in varied pulsations, and the pipe and flute among the grass and seabent on the down, and the hiss of the sand-grains that were caught and turned over and rolled along in the bare patches. Near the extreme verge of the precipice, where the soil was crumbly, and a false step would plunge into destruction, the sheep were lying at ease, dozing, waking now and then, and approaching the sweet grass to nibble, then going back to the edge of the precipice to sleep again ; for the sheep have ascertained that, with a wind on shore, the edge of the cliff is the most shel-

tered spot ; the wind, hurling itself against the
crag, is beaten upwards and curls over, and falls
further inland, just as might a wave. Consequently, in a heavy gale, partial stillness of air
is found at the cliff edge.

Josephine wore a dark-blue dress, and over
her head was a handkerchief, pinned beneath
her chin. Bessie lay, silent in her lap, with her
head on Josephine's bosom, and her thin-drawn
face looking seaward. Josephine also was silent;
she also was looking seaward. Her face was
greatly changed since we first saw her on the
lightship. Then she was girlish, with mischief
and defiance in her splendid eyes, and life glow-
ing in her veins, showing through her olive skin,
Then, there was promise in her of a handsome
woman, full of spirit and self-will; of a clever
woman, who could keep a circle of men about
her, charmed, yet wincing, at her wit and
humour. But the Josephine who sat on the
bench of the 'Magpie' was not the same. The
promise was unfulfilled. The girlishness was
gone. The self-confidence had made way for
timidity; the defiance in her great dark eyes
was exchanged for appeal. There was no more
mischief lurking anywhere, in the eyes, in the
dimples of the cheek, in the curve of the lips;
but there was an amount of nobleness, and
mixed with gentleness, great resolution, marked

in all the features. It was like the nature of
that west wind that she inhaled—strong yet
tender, direct yet infinitely soft, soothing, heal-
ing, loving, strengthening—and pure.

Josephine had gone through a long ordeal,
to which she had subjected herself, and from
which there seemed no issue. Spiritually,
morally, it had done her good; but it had not
advanced her towards that end which she
sought—at least so it seemed to her. She was
no nearer to Richard Cable than she had been.
If he conferred on her a boon, it was in such a
manner as to rob it of all the grace of a gift,
and of all the hope it might carry.

What a fascination there is in looking at
the sea! Even the most vulgar soul is affected
by it. On the sea-border we are on the frontier
of the infinite. The sight of the ocean is like
the sound of music calling forth the soul from
the thoughts of to-day, from its cage-life to
freedom, and an unutterable yearning after what
is not—the Perfect. At the sight of the sea, all
the aspirations long down-trodden, long forgotten, lift up their hands again, and stretch out of
the dust of sordid life. All the sorrows of the
past, scarred over, break out and bleed again,
the blood running down, drop by drop, warm,
soothing, yet painful. All the generous thoughts
that have been pared down and disfigured into

mean acts, shake off their disguise, reassume their original dignity, and master us. All the unrealities, the affectations, which have bound us about, break away, and we stand forth fresh and natural and true. All the selfishness, the contraction of interest to one miserable point, discovers its unworthiness, and the heart swells with a charity that has no bounds.

I have seen those who have taken novels out on the downs to read, sit hour by hour looking seaward, with the novel unread on the lap. The sea was the great reality, the infinite truth waking up in their minds a thousand thoughts and emotions, drawing them out, withering the base, and bracing the true. It showed them in their own selves all the elements of the noblest romance; it revealed to them the true hero or heroine, in themselves, in the ideal, towards which they should ever strive, and in the pursuit of which work out the grandest of romances, which is not a romance, but a great reality.

So Josephine sat looking seaward, and thinking without knowing that she thought, and on her lap lay little Bessie thinking, as her eyes looked seaward, and not knowing that she was thinking. In Goethe's ballad the Erle-king calls to the child, uttering promises; and the father who bears the child does not hear the voice, and shudders at the thought that his child may be lured away. The sea—the infinite sea, called to the child and to her who held the child with a voice that both heard—a voice full of promise, but full of mystery as to what it promised.

The bench on which Josephine sat was made of old wreck-timber, and at the sides stood the curved ribs of a ship or boat, meeting overhead, and boarded in, so as to form a rude arbour. The sides cut off the wind, when it did not blow directly on shore, and the seat was a meeting-place for the coastguard. As Josephine sat here, a man came round the corner of the house and approached the place where she sat. She did not see him because of the planks that framed in the seat. Five minutes after, another man appeared in like manner round the other angle of the house, and came towards her arbour, and he also was unseen as he drew nigh, for the same reason. The first who came was Richard Cable, and he came to see Bessie. As already said. he had not been to the 'Magpie' since she had been there; but of late a great uneasiness had come over him. He remembered what his mother had said, as he moved to Red Windows—-that he laid his foundations in his first-born, and set up the gates in his youngest. In his troubled mind the fancy rose that he had

lost his first-born—her love, at least, by thwart-
ing her, and ruined her happiness ; and that he
was about to lose his poor little Bessie in another
way. He had struggled against this impression,
against his desire to see her, how she was pro·
gressing, to assure himself that the fear that
weighed on him was unfounded. At length he
had ridden over ; and having heard of Mrs.
Corye that Josephine was with the child on the
bench, he went in search of her ; very reluctant
to meet Josephine, and very desirous to see his
child. He stood screened by the side of the
bench, gray wooden wreck-timber planks,
carved over with initials, listening for Bessie's
voice, waiting for her to run out on the down,
when he would go after her, catch her up in his
arms, and carry her off, without having to face
Josephine.

At first he doubted whether those he sought
were there ; but there was a round knot-hole
in one of the planks, and on looking through
that, he saw Josephine, and the little girl leaning on her bosom. Josephine's profile was
clean cut against the sky, noble, fine, and
beautiful ; but he could not see from that
silhouette how changed the face was. As he
thus stood now looking through the hole at
Josephine and Bessie, then, caught by the
fascination of the sea, looking out seaward,

losing himself in dreams full of trouble and pain and froth and brine, there passed a flicker of sunlight over the rolling ocean, like a skein of floss-silk of the purest white blown along the gray surface, and caught and spread by the inequalities, and then lifted and carried on again by the wind. He looked at this till it disappeared, and as he looked, his sense of time passed away, and he knew not how long he had been standing there, unable to muster courage to present himself before those who sat so near him and yet were parted from him. As he thus stood, leaning back against the wall, another man came round the house, from the opposite side, and ensconced himself on the other side of the arbour. This was Mr. Cornellis. He had driven up to the 'Magpie' five minutes after the arrival of Cable, and had inquired for Josephine, not by name, but as 'the young person staying here with one of Cable's children.' He had been to St. Kerian, and had there learned where she was and what she was doing; and had come on to the 'Magpie' after her. But as he had heard from Mrs. Corye that Richard had himself gone in the same direction a few minutes before, he contented himself with slipping round the corner and planting himself beside the bench, screened by the side, where he thought he might stand unobserved and hear what took place before he showed himself.

So Josephine sat on the old bench with the ribs of a wreck arching over her, planked in on both sides, and the sick child on her lap, both silent, both lost in a day-dream; and on each side of her, unknown to her, stood a man with whom she was intimately allied, and yet from both of whom she was widely parted —her father and her husband. She knew nothing of their proximity; she had not heard their steps on the turf; and the wind that blew into the arbour, filled it and whirled about in it, and hummed and piped and broke out into song, and sank into sobs, and pulled at the timbers, making them creak, and sought out their rifts, to whistle through them, so that she could hear no slight sound outside that rude orchestral shell.

Mr. Cornellis leaned back against the wall, with his hands behind him, as a protection to his coat, and looked out to sea; but on him, on him alone of the four, the fascination had no power. The same wondrous expanse, the same travelling glories and obscurities, the same mysterious depths and distances, and glimpses into further far-away, and screens veiling the far off, the same call of the many-voiced ocean in one great harmonious song—passing over

the mind of Mr. Cornellis, not even as a breath
over a mirror that leaves a momentary trace—
it affected him not at all, for the faculty was
dead in him, if it had ever existed—the faculty
of responding to the hidden things of nature.
One deep calleth to another deep, sang David,
sitting on the hill-slope of Bethlehem, looking
away west to the Mediterranean, as the sight
of the sea woke in his soul a consciousness of
the Divine, of the Eternal; and the deep sea
still calls to the deep in every human soul that
has depth; only to the shallow puddles does it
call in vain.

Where the planks were joined on the side
where stood Mr. Cornellis, a little rift remained.
The planks had not fitted originally, or had
warped after having been nailed to the stan-
chions. Through this cleft he looked, and he
could see his daughter. He could not see the
face of the child on her bosom; but he saw
the head over her arm, and the golden hair
in dimpled waves flowing down upon Josephine's
dark-blue dress, and the parting on the top of
the head, and just a strip of white brow.

Then both men heard the clear, beautiful
voice of Josephine raised in song:

O wie wogt es, wie wogt es, so schön auf der Fluth!

and looking in, saw her swaying the sick Bessie
in her arms to the rhythm of the melody.

Cable saw more—he saw the delicate, transparent hand of his child raised, stroking the cheek of her nurse, and then—the song of the Mermaid was interrupted as Josephine turned her lips and kissed the little hand.

Josephine did not continue the song, but said : 'Bessie, can you kneel up on my lap, and let me tell you something?'

The child did not answer in words; she had become very silent of late—the closeness, the reserve of her father was showing itself as an inherited characteristic in her. But though she did not speak, she acted; she raised her head, put her hands on Josephine's shoulders, and knelt on her lap, opposite her, still resting a hand on each shoulder of her nurse. The wind blew in, took her golden hair and swept it forward towards the face of Josephine; and Josephine was obliged to make her hold her head away, lest the hair should spread itself over her face and obscure her eyes and prevent her from speaking.

'My dear Bessie,' she said in a voice full of gentleness and sweetness, and with a tremble in it that now never left it, 'I must tell you something. I cannot let you coax me, and pat my cheek and kiss me, as you so often do, without your knowing to whom you show this love.'

Then Cable's brows knitted. Josephine was going to betray the trust imposed on her, to tell the child that she was her stepmother, and to implant in Bessie's mind the suspicion that her father had been unjust to one who was kind and good. He took a step forward to leave his hiding-place and prevent the disclosure; but he thought better of his resolution, and desisted. He must not provoke a scene which would agitate his child.

'Bessie,' said Josephine, 'I do not think your father would wish you to be so dear and sweet to me, to let me think you loved me, and remain in ignorance of what should be told.'

'She is false also,' thought Cable; 'she *knows* I do not wish it.'

'My darling,' continued Josephine, 'look me full in the face—look with your blue eyes straight into mine, whilst I tell you something, and I shall be able to read in your eyes what you think.' She paused, and drew a long breath. 'You know, my pretty pet,' said Josephine, 'how you suffer in your back, how that you have always—that is, since you can remember—been a sickly child; that you have not been able to play with your sisters like those who are strong; that you have had much pain to bear, and many sleepless nights. You know that now you are very weak and soon tired, and you do not care to talk much or take exercise, but to lie quiet on my breast and look at the sea. My dear, I also like to look at the sea ; and the sea has been talking to me, and telling me to be true—always true, and deal openly, and never hide what should be known, and reap what has not been sown by me. That is why I want to tell you this thing now, which has been kept secret from you. Do you know why you are infirm and in pain, with a suffering life instead of a life joyous and painless?'

'I do not know,' said Bessie.

'No one has told you?'

The child shook her head, and as she did so, the wind caught her yellow hair and wrapped it about her face, so that she was obliged to let go her hold of Josephine's shoulder with one hand, to thrust back her curls behind her ears.

'May I have your blue kerchief with the white spots,' asked Bessie, 'to tie over my head? The hair blows into my eyes, and I cannot see you.'

Then Josephine unknotted the kerchief from her own head—the knot was under her chin—and tied it over the golden head of little Bessie. How was it that, in some dim way, the sight of that blue white-spotted kerchief was familiar to Richard? 'It is an old pocket-

handkerchief of your father's,' said Josephine,
'and covers you best, as his love is spread over
your head—not over mine.'

Then Richard remembered the handkerchief, and the mockery with which once
Josephine had spoken of it.

'When your father left Hanford, where he
once lived—that was when you were quite a
baby, and you remember nothing about it—
then he left this kerchief behind, and I have
kept it ever since.'

'Were you there then?'

'Yes.'

'Why did papa leave that place for St.
Kerian?'

'Because, in the first place, the cottage at
St. Kerian came to him from your great-uncle;
and in the next, he had very painful associations with Hanford.'

'You knew him there?'

'Yes—and it was there that happened the
sad accident which has made you a sufferer.'

Cruel, cruel Josephine! always wounding!
She was about now to tell his daughter how
he had let her fall when he was drunk, and so
to turn away the child's heart from him. Thus
were his mother's words likely to come true;
he had thrown away the heart of his eldest,
and the heart of his youngest was to be

plucked from him. He set his elbow against the wall, and his fingers he thrust through his hair, and he looked with eyes that gleamed with remorse and anger through the knot-hole at Josephine.

Then she went on, in her low voice, that quivered as sunlight on the surface of water : ' Look me well in the face, dear Bessie, and do not take your eyes off mine. You shall know the truth now, from my lips. The reason why you have a bad back and an un-happy life is this—that you were let fall on a hard stone floor, when you were a baby, and your bones soft and not full set. That is the secret that has not been told you. You were born sound and strong as Mary and Jane and Effie and Martha, and the rest ; and now you would be able to run about like the rest, and be strong, and have no pain, but for that fall. —Well ? ' The great brown eyes of Josephine looked into the blue eyes of the child, inquir-ingly. ' Have you nothing to ask ? Do you not want to know where the guilt lies of ruin-ing all your sweet and precious life ? '

Bessie shook her head, and her golden hair did not flutter, but the end of the blue, white-spotted kerchief, with R. C. marked on it, flapped in the wind.

The brow of Cable was drawn and corded

like rope, and his knees shook under him with convulsive agitation. Should he now step forth at this supreme moment, and arrest the word on the heartless, venomous woman's mouth?

Then in the same low, quivering tones, but yet so clear that Richard lost not one word, Josephine went on: 'It was my doing, Bessie. I—and I alone am to blame for all your suffering; and that is also why your father left Hanford—to take you away from me.'

Not a wink, not a contraction of the iris in the child's blue orbs.

'Some one,' said Josephine, 'said to me that when you were told this you would hate me, and raise your little fists and beat my eyes till they were blind with blood and tears.'

Then little Bessie let go her hold of Josephine's shoulders, and threw her arms about her neck, and platted the white fingers in her dark hair, and kissed her passionately on the eyes, and then laid her little head on one of Josephine's shoulders, and looked up into her eyes and said: 'But—I am glad it was you, and I love you a thousand times better.'

Out seaward was a long, hard-edged, black roller coming on to the shore, looking as black and hard as the iron rocks against which it was about to fling itself. But at one point the crest broke and turned into foam; at another

point far away in the same wave-crest, another
white foam-head appeared ; and from each side
the foam ran inward, and it seemed as if they
must meet and turn the whole long wave into
one white breaker. But no ! There heaved up
between the approaching lines of foam a yeasty
heap of water, into which the advancing wave
dissolved, and lost its continuity. Richard
looked seaward at this roller. Little matters
determine our actions in moments of indecision.
Had the foam-lines met, he would have stepped
forward, and an immediate reconciliation might
have ensued. But the failure in the wave
broke down the dawning desire for reunion, and
he stole away back to the inn without a word.

As he left, Mr. Cornellis stood forth, and
saw him go, and in another moment confronted
his daughter and Bessie. But Cable went into
the 'Magpie' and ordered his horse. Then
said Mrs. Corye to him : 'I suppose you can't
carry a parcel ? The young woman has done
all the seven confirmation dresses, and they
are tied up in a parcel, ready to be sent to
St. Kerian.'

'Give them to me,' said Cable ; 'I will
take them in front of my saddle.'

When Josephine caught sight of her father,
she sprang up with a cry of pleasure, and with
a flushed face, placed Bessie on the seat and

ran to him with outstretched arms. She was
so poverty-stricken in love, that she hailed
with delight the appearance of one to whom
she was tied with the tenderest bands. 'O
papa! how kind of you to come and see me!
Oh! how is dear Aunt Judith? I have not
seen her for so long, and I do love her so! O
papa! this is a pleasure.' She held his hand in
both hers and wrung it, and kissed it and wept
with delight.

'I have come to fetch you home,' said Mr.
Cornellis. 'Your Aunt Judith is expecting you,
and I want you.'

'Papa!' exclaimed Josephine suddenly,
'you are in mourning—deep mourning. What
has happened?'

'My dear, I have lost my wife. You know
that I married Miss Otterbourne, who was
twenty years older than myself. She has not
lived long. The complete change in the modes
of life, after she had settled into old-maidish
ways, broke her up very quickly.'

'O papa, papa! And where are you now?'

'At Bewdley, my dear.'

'But that goes to Captain Sellwood.'

'Not at all. She had free disposal of her
property, and she has left everything to me.'

'But—it is not fair.'

'I do not ask your opinion in this matter,'

he said coldly; 'I have come to fetch you home. Judith is getting old and failing, and I want you to manage the house.'

'But—papa—I cannot leave.'

'Why not? Richard Cable will have nothing to say to you. Has he given you the least encouragement?'

She was silent.

'Do you know that he overheard all that passed between you and the child just now? Had he desired a reconciliation he would have sought it. He did not. He never will. Give up this absurd and hopeless Don Quixote pursuit, and come with me. I am now very well off. You were at Bewdley as a servant; you come back as mistress. I have packed off the worthless crew of domestics and hangers-on who preyed on the old lady. Come back with me. You have done more than was necessary to satisfy that fellow Cable; and as he still rejects you, show him proper pride, and leave him to himself.'

'Papa!'—she breathed fast—'you are rich now?'

'Yes, very.'

'Then, oh, do repay the insurance.'

He gave her a look, so evil, so full of rage and malice, that she turned sharply about to see Bessie.

He did not speak again; he went away without another word or look, and left without a parting message through the hostess.

Not so Cable.

When Josephine came in, Mrs. Corye pointed to the table, on which something was scrawled in chalk. 'Look there,' she said. 'He—I mean Cable—wrote that for you, and when you've read it, wipe it out.'

On the table was inscribed: 'Thursday—bring Bessie. Friday—confirmation.' That was all.

## CHAPTER LVII.

### THE FOUNDATION.

RICHARD CABLE scarcely slept all night. He thought of many things. He thought of what he had seen and overheard at Pentargon. He saw in the darkness the arms of his child round the neck, interlaced with the hair of Josephine, her head tied up in his blue white-spotted kerchief, lying on her shoulder, looking up into the pale face of her nurse, with a soul of love and forgiveness streaming out of those blue eyes. But he thought of something beside—of the plan he had made for Mary; and he was by no means sure that she would be well content with the arrangement. One circumstance had, however, occurred to make his way easier. When a young man has been refused, his self-love receives a wound more severe than his heart, and he is then impelled to do some act which will retrieve his lost self-respect. A man who has been refused, or jilted, is ready to propose to the next girl he sees; and no

sooner was Walter Penrose aware that his suit
for Mary Cable was unacceptable, than he
offered himself to Sarah Jones. He did not
care particularly for Sarah; but he did not
choose to have it thought in the place that he
was a rejected lover; and he did not choose
that the Cables should consider him as incon-
solable. As this engagement was hurried, the
wedding was also hurried; Sarah Jones had no
desire to let Walter slip through her fingers
by delay, and Walter wished to have his fate
settled irrevocably as speedily as possible, out
of defiance to the Cables, who had slighted his
pretensions.

After breakfast one morning, Richard Cable
said to Mary: ‘Child, when you have cleared
away, come to me into the summer-house; I
have a word to say to you of some import-
ance.’

‘Father, I hear the bishop arrives to-
morrow.’

‘Yes; but I am not going to speak to you
about the bishop.’

‘And the confirmation is on Friday.’

‘Yes; I suppose so; but that is not the
matter.’

He saw her and Martha exchange looks.
Martha put up her lip and looked sulky.
Martha had inherited her father's stubbornness.

She and Mary clung to each other, as the twins who intervened between Mary and her were fast friends and inseparable. Martha looked up to Mary with passionate love, regarded her as the most beautiful and perfect girl in the world; fought her battles, resented every slight shown her, or supposed slight, as she would bridle with pride and pleasure at every acknowledgment of her sister's excellence.

Cable went to his summer-house and smoked a pipe. Before he had finished it, he heard a timid foot on the gravel, and in another moment Mary stood in the open door.

'Come in,' said Cable. 'What is the matter? Upset because you have broken a plate? Bah! Fourpence will set that to rights. Come inside, Mary dear; I must have a serious word with you.'

She entered, trembling, and with changing colour, changing as fast as the flushes in the evening clouds. Tears sparkled on her eyelashes, as raindrops on fern-leaves in the hedges at morn.

'What is the matter, child? Why are you frightened? Your father will never do anything to displease you. You can rely on that. His whole care is for your happiness, and it is for your happiness that he is now arranging.'

She raised her blue eyes; they were swimming with tears, so full of tears that he could not read through the watery veil what they said. He could not say for a moment any more. His pipe did not draw as it should; he unscrewed it and blew through the nozzle. His blood throbbed in his temples. He was vexed with his mother because she had refused to speak to Mary about his purpose, and relieve him of the irksome obligation. 'Mary,' he said, after a long pause, during which she stood before him with folded hands and lowered eyes — 'Mary, I suppose you have formed a rough guess what my business is with you?'

She made no answer with her lips. Had he looked up, he might have read the reply in the pain-twitching lips of his child and in her shifting colour.

'Can you give a guess of what I have to say?'

Then she held up her head, looked full through her tears in her father's face, and answered: 'Yes, dear father, I know—I can guess what you want to—to say. But—O father! father dearest—spare me this time—do not say it.'

'Spare you this time?' echoed Cable. What is the meaning of these words? When

have I not been considerate and kind to you—
to you above the rest?'

No answer.

He waited; but as he received no reply,
without looking in her face, he began again:
'Mary.'

'Father,' she said, 'let me——' But her
voice failed her, and she put her hands over
her eyes.

'You do not know what is good for you,
my child,' he said. 'You are indeed still very
young, scarcely eighteen, and yet—— But
never mind; your mother was married early.
If I have doubted for a moment whether I
acted rightly on a former occasion, my doubts
have vanished to-day. That young fellow, who
once took a fancy to you, is now——Hark!'

At that moment the bells of the parish
church began a glad peal. The wedding service was over that united Walter Penrose with
Sarah Jones, and the ringers were sending the
welcome from the church tower.

Then Mary raised her hands, clasped them
over her head, uttering a piercing cry, and
sank at her father's feet: 'Father! O my
father! you have killed me!'

Cable caught her, and tried to raise her;
but she twisted herself from his hands, and on
her knees staggered round the summer-house,

clasping her ears, to shut out the reverberation of the wedding bells.

Cable went after her ; he caught her in his arms and held her ; but she slipped down on the floor again and lay her length on it, beating the floor with her head, as one mad, and then scrambling up on her knees and throwing herself in a heap in the corner. 'O father! my father!' she cried, 'this is your doing! Walter does not love any one but me ; and I—I love, and can love none other. I shall never, never marry now! You have made me miserable— you have broken my heart.'

Richard Cable was as a man turned to stone. He could not speak; he tried, but his voice failed. He put his hand to his brow, and a deep groan escaped his breast. All at once he stood up ; he could not breathe in the summer-house. He was stunned by the reverberation of those St. Kerian bells, beating in upon his brain, from all the eight sides of his wooden house. He left Mary kneeling on the ground ; he rushed forth. He opened his gate and hobbled down the road. He could not bear to face his children. He did not feel the ground under his feet ; he was like a dreamer, falling, falling, touching nothing. The birds sang in the bushes, the holly leaves reflected the sun from their shining leaves on the hedge. Everything swam about him. He could not run because of his thigh, and he had not his stick, so he went painfully, lurching like a drunken man. He had pierced his best loved daughter's heart; he had robbed her of her happiness, alienated her from him for ever—he had laid the foundation in his first-born.

Whither was he going? He did not know himself. He wanted to be away from Red Windows, somewhere out of the sound of Mary's sobs, away from the reproachful eyes of her sisters; somewhere where he might be alone in his misery. There was one spot to which instinctively he gravitated—the old cob cottage. He did not consider that it had been given up to Josephine, or if he thought of that, he remembered she was away, and that, though she dwelt in it, it was now vacant. He did not rest till he reached it. The key was kept in the same secret place, the hole in the thatch, and when he put his hand there, he found the key. He opened the door and went in. He did not look about him; he saw the old armchair in the old place, and the table and the seven stools. The hearth was cold; the room was still, only a few flies humming in it. There were a few trifles that belonged to Josephine on the chimney-shelf and on the table; and to a crook in the ceiling hung a bunch of pink everlastings, head downward. He threw himself into the old chair, and folded his arms on his knees, and laid his head on his arms and wept.

How long he sat there he did not know; thoughts hot as molten metal flowed white and glaring through his brain. Had he been happy in Red Windows? Was he not more miserable in his wealth than he had been in his poverty? What had his money done for him but steal his children's hearts from him, and seal up his perception of what was for their welfare? There, round the table, were the stools of his children, on which they had sat as little things, and eaten their frugal meals. How much better they had tasted seasoned with love, than the richer repasts at Red Windows strewn with verjuice.

Those bells! Those wedding bells were still ringing! Oh, what a happy day for him, had they rung for Mary's wedding! How content he might have been with her down in St. Kerian, near the smithy. Then every day he would have strolled into the village to see her and talk with the smith, his son-in-law. Now that was over. Mary's heart was broken. The bright future of the dearest being he loved had been dashed to pieces by his hand. Could she ever forgive him—him who had spoiled her entire future, blighted her whole life? How could he live in the same house with her whose happiness he had wrecked?

Then he remembered what he had witnessed on the cliff behind the ' Magpie '—he saw again the little head bound up in his blue kerchief, resting on Josephine's shoulder, looking up into her face, and saying: ' I am glad it was you, and I love you a thousand times better!'

O wondrous beauty of forgiveness! St. Luke's summer in the moral world, when a soft glory illumines the fading leaves and drooping vegetation, and makes the touch of decay and death seem the touch of perfect loveliness.

What was the worm at the root of all Cable's happiness, that which had robbed all his successes of satisfaction? Was it not the bitterness with which he had thought of Josephine, the savage determination with which he had stamped out every spark of relenting love, that had for a moment twinkled in his gloomy heart?

As he thus thought, he groaned. Then, suddenly, he was roused and touched by a hand. He looked up, bewildered. Jacob Corye the innkeeper stood before him with agitated, mottled face.

' You've heard it? It is true! We are all done for.'

Cable could not collect his senses at first.

R 2

'I came over at once, the moment the news reached me. I went up to Red Windows. Then I heard you had gone down the lane. Some one saw you come on here. I followed. Is it true? Tell me what you have heard. My God! this is frightful.'

'I do not understand you.'

'The Duchy Bank has failed—stopped payment. I had three thousand five hundred pounds in it. And you——?'

'Everything,' answered Cable.

'Just heard it. Could hardly believe it. I came over here. It is a frightful loss to me. Three thousand five hundred pounds! Why, I can never start the "Champagne Air Hotel."'

'It is my ruin,' said Cable. 'I owe money for Red Windows, and I have put my savings into shares in the bank as portions for my girls.' He put his hands over his brow and laughed fiercely. 'Naked came I into the world, and naked I shall go out. The Lord gave and the Lord hath taken away; but I cannot and I will not say, Blessed be the name of the Lord.'

'Three thousand five hundred pounds!' groaned Corye. 'That takes pints of blood out of one's veins.'

'I am bled to death,' said Cable.

'Look here! What will become of Red Windows?'

'It will be sold over my head. I have not paid off; and I am a shareholder.'

'You have everything in the bank?'

'Every penny.'

'Look here, Uncle Dick,' said Corye. 'Under these circumstances, we must give up the "Champagne Air Hotel."'

'Yes.'

'And we must think no more of mating my Joshua and your Mary.'

'That is past,' said Cable.

'Three thousand five hundred pounds!' groaned Jacob. 'Well, I pity you. I can feel. I am cruel badly bitten.' Then he went away.

Richard Cable remained in the same position and in the same place. He did not return to Red Windows for his dinner. He sat, stunned with despair, rocking himself in his armchair, looking upon the white ashes of his first life, and the ashes of his second life. His first ambition had been realised, and had turned to dust when he grasped it. The second had been realised, and had failed him also. What was done could not be undone. He must return with his daughters to the poor cob cottage. The wealth was gone as a dream—not a happy dream—a dream of disappointed ambition, of pride unsatisfied. It would have been better for him and his children if he had never left his stone-breaking, never separated himself from them. That episode of prosperity, like the episode of marriage with Josephine, had done nothing for him except unfit him for the life he had been accustomed to lead. He felt inclined in his misery to take his stone-breaker's hammer and break his daughters' hearts with it, one after another, and then die himself. Red Windows must be abandoned, and they must all accommodate themselves as best they could to the cottage, and cultivate again the three-cornered garden; and he must go along his rounds with the van of calves and droves of young stock, rebuilding slowly his broken-down fortune.

' Cursed be the day,' muttered Cable, ' that ever I dreamed that daring dream ! '

His head was burning. He could not weep now ; his eyes were fireballs. The fountain of tears in his heart was dry as an old cistern, and nothing lay at the bottom but grit and canker. One thing that embittered his misfortune most of all to him was the thought of how the St. Kerian folk, whom he had held aloof from, would rejoice over his misfortune. Those who had most fawned on him in his prosperity would

now turn their heel upon him. How Penrose
the blacksmith that day would laugh over his
ill-luck, and bless his stars that his Walter had
escaped union with one whom misfortune followed! How Tregurtha, from whom he had
purchased Summerleaze, would rub his hands,
and vow that the day had now come which he
had long foretold, when Uncle Dick's pride
would be brought low!

Then the strength of Richard Cable's character began to manifest itself again, as these
galling visions presented themselves before him.
It was true that he was a ruined man; but he
had still the brains and the skill to make a new
fortune by following the same course he had
already pursued. As he began to think of the
future, the present lost its intensity of bitterness. He felt that he still had in him sufficient
energy to begin life for the third time; but he
was shaken, and he could never hope to recover
all that was now taken from him. There were
other competitors stepping in where he had
shown the way.

Whilst thus thinking, he heard the door
open, and the blacksmith, Penrose, came in.
'Well, Uncle Dicky,' said the smith, 'what be
this bad news I've heard? The Duchy Bank
gone scatt [broken] and all your savings lost?'

Cable nodded and sighed.

'Bless me,' said Penrose, 'that's a bad look-out for you. Have you laid nothing by elsewhere?'

Cable shook his head.

'By the powers!' said the blacksmith, 'I'm mighty sorry for you. I've been at the wedding of my boy, and I'm only sorry he weren't spliced to the other one. Your Mary would have suited me better than Sarah Jones. But it was not to be; so let the past lie covered with leaves. Sarah Jones brings some money with her; but she has a shrewish temper, if what folks say be true. I'd rather have had your Mary without a penny than Sarah with all her brass. But there! what is done is done, and to-day the parson has hammered them together on the anvil, and there'll be no parting after that, whether they agree or not. As for her sharp tongue, he must learn to put up with it and turn its point with gentleness.'

Cable sighed and thought of his marriage with Josephine.

'Well, Uncle Dick,' continued Penrose, 'I've just seen Jacob Corye, who is badly hit. But he says you are worse bitten than he, and that there was nothing left for you and your maidens but the workhouse.'

Cable looked up ironically and said: 'No, not that.'

'No,' pursued the blacksmith; 'I knew it could not be so bad as that. Still, I thought I'd come on and see.—Corye said you were here taking on dreadfully about your loss, and like to do yourself an injury. Then an idea came into my head; it flashed up like a spark on red-hot iron. I came on, and here I find you.'

'Yes,' said Cable, 'here you find me.' He was not angry with Penrose for his intrusion. He felt that it was kindly meant, and the sympathy of the blacksmith touched him.

'Now, harky' to me,' said the blacksmith, lowering his voice. 'I know you well enough —a straight man as ever was. I reckon I'm a straight man too; and where I'm crooked, may God Almighty hammer me out of my crookedness with the hammer of adversity, straight again! But there—I've come to say that I've a matter of a couple of hundred pounds lying idle—thank heaven, not in a bank, but in my old woman's nightcap, and stuffed up the chimney in our bedroom—all in gold, and you're heartily welcome to the loan of it as long as you like. You leave this door unlocked to-night, and I'll come along as if I were out to smoke and blow off the drink I've had to take because of all the toasts and well-wishings, being my son's wedding day; and I'll come in here, nobody seeing, and I'll put the old woman's nightcap and its contents into thicky [yonder] oven, where you'll find it to-morrow morning, and nobody the wiser.—No words,' said Penrose, starting up. 'I reckon I hear steps coming. I'm wanted because the young people are off.'

Before Cable could recover his speech, for moved to the loss of words he was, Penrose was gone. At the same moment in came three other men, Tregurtha the farmer, Bonithon the saddler, and Hoskins the miller. Each looked at his fellow to speak. Tregurtha, nudged by the saddler and the miller, after a few ineffectual whispered remonstrances, came sheepishly forward. 'You're in the old nest again, Uncle Dicky,' he began, then coughed. 'Us three chaps were in the "Silver Bowl" just now, when Jacob Corye came, mighty took on about the loss of his money through the break of the Duchy Bank. He told us as how you had lost everything—as you'd put all the fortune you had into the Duchy, and took it out of calves and bullocks. I reckon it were a mistake. Keep your money in flesh, say I. I once lost a power of money in law. I never went to law again after that. It taught me a lesson, and I've profited by it. That is why I've money now. You may lose a calf here or a cow there

of milk-fever, or a horse with the glanders, or
a pig with the measles—and talking of that, my
wife's cruel bad wi' erysipelas—but you've
other things to fall back on. It is not so with
a bank ; that's like the bridge in the nursery
story, which when it bended, there the story
ended. Well, old friend, we—that is, Ephraim
Bonithon, and Tony Hoskins, and I—was very
troubled when we heard you had got pixy-led
in Queer Lane ; so, when Corye was gone, we
put our heads together. Now, us three—that's
Tony Hoskins, and Ephraim Bonithon, and I—
have all of us got money laid by, are warmish
men in our way —the thermometer in us don't
go down to zero. So we've come to say, if you
want to get on in the cattle business and are
pinched to start with again, we three—that is
to say, me, and Ephraim Bonithon, and Tony
Hoskins—be ready to stand security for you to
any sum in reason that you like to name.—
And,' continued Tregurtha, ' don't you never
go for to think and suppose of selling Red
Windows. Us of St. Kerian be proud of that
house standing up above the town, and us shows
it to the little 'uns as a visible lesson to 'em of
what uprightness and energy and perseverance
may perform. Moreover—and besides '—he
took breath after this word—' us three men,
the afore-in-mentioned Tony Hoskins, and me,

and Ephraim Bonithon, can't abear to think of them seven shining and adorning beauties, your sweet maidens, God bless 'em! should not be housed in a nest worthy of such treasures. Then therefore and because'—another long breath—'if the creditors dare to sell that there house over your head, then we three—that is, Ephraim Bonithon, Tony Hoskins, and I, say —damn their eyes! And we'll buy the house and make it over to you, to repay us as you earn the money.' Then he drew a long breath and said 'There!' and the other two drew the backs of their hands across their noses and grunted 'There!'

Then suddenly, panting, in the doorway, stood little Lettice, who cried: 'O father! come, come quick! Who do you think is come to Red Windows? The Bishop and Mrs. Sellwood; and they say they are old friends of yours; and want to see you and us all—and are asking after little Bessie.—And,' after panting a while, ' the bishop has brought a to-day's paper, from Launceston, and he says it's all a parcel of lies about the Duchy Bank; it's the other bank, the name I can't call to mind, is broken, and not the Duchy.'

Then Richard Cable held out his hands and clasped and shook those of Ephraim Bonithon, William Tregurtha, and Anthony Hoskins, shook and squeezed them, but said nothing; yet, as he hurried away, his body shook, and his breast heaved convulsively, and sounds issued from his mouth, that made Tregurtha say : ' By George, he is pleased—how he is laughing ! '

But Lettice, looking up in her father's face as she ran at his side, asked : ' Papa, why are you crying ? '

Then he said in a choking voice : ' Run, Lettice, run after Mr. Corye, and tell him not to fail to send little Bessie and—*her* who is with Bessie, in his gig, to Red Windows, to-morrow.'

# CHAPTER LVIII.

### PIXY-LED.

'LOOKY' here, Joshua,' said Mr. Jacob Corye, as his son was getting the trap ready on Thursday, in which to take Josephine and Bessie to St. Kerian. 'As the Duchy Bank isn't broke, you make yourself uncommon sweet to Mary Cable, and tell the father that I'm game to go on with "Champagne Air Hotel."—Lord! what a shock it gave me when I heard the news; and however it got about is a wonder. If folks tell news, why do they always twist it so as to stick in your ribs? I've heard one of the coastguard tell, who was in Burmah, how the natives there run amuck. They get a sword or a spike, or something onpleasant, and they run along as hard as a racer, skewering every one they meet with it. It be just the same in England with folks; if only they get hold of a nasty, sharp, spiky bit of news, they run amuck with that out of pure wickedness.'

'Father, the sky looks ugly.'

'Yes; I reckon we shall have dirty weather; Northern Nannies,[1] maybe, drifts of storm and hail; but they'll pass.—What horse are you putting in?'

'Dancing Jenny.'

'Why Dancing Jenny? She cuts capers in the shafts.'

'You had Derby yesterday to ride over to St. Kerian on; and Dancing Jenny wants a run to take the tingle out of her toes.'

'If you was going alone; but with two fragile bits o' womankind, I should say put in Whiteface.'

'Whiteface has no life in him. Leave me alone. Do you think I can't drive? Why, you might set me to manage an Australian buck-jumper, and I'd do it.'

His father shrugged his shoulders. 'Well, put on a honey-face yourself to Mary Cable, mind you, now that the Duchy Bank is not broke. Get your mother to look at your face before you start, to see that it wears a proper amiable smile.'

There was no parish or other road to St. Kerian from Pentargon, because Pentargon was a bay, and not a village; and the road along the cliffs as far as where the artery of commu-

---

[1] A 'Northern Nanny' is a cold storm of hail and wind from the north.

nication between St. Kerian and the coast entered it, nearly doubled the distance. As the crow flew, and as the track ran for foot-passengers and horsemen, the distance was seven miles; but this lay across moor and between bogs, and only those who knew it could venture along it. The neighbourhood was sparsely populated, and the traffic was small, except along the main turnpike roads. Near the coast, the slate rocks, laden with carboniferous particles that give them a black colour, rise abruptly, but much contorted from the sea; they fall away inland, forming dips, in which are swamps, where rise numerous affluents of the Tamar; and beyond this boggy district extend granite ridges and moors in a chain, forming the spine of the Cornish peninsula. Such population as exists clusters in the valleys and by the sea; the moors are left to solitude and desolation. The short-cut to St. Kerian lay across one of the sedgy marshy basins in the slate, and then over a spur of granite moor, beneath which nestled St. Kerian in verdure and shelter from the sea-gales.

Mr. Joshua Corye had no idea of going round by the road; the ugly look of the sky made him desirous of getting the journey over as quickly as possible; and Dancing Jenny would be less likely to cut her capers among ruts and swamps than on a broad, macadamised highway.

When the gig was ready, Dancing Jenny began to paw and spring and show the antics that gave her her name; and little Bessie was frightened, and shrank to the side of Josephine.

'Are you wise, Joshua,' said his father, 'putting Jenny in that cart? The shafts are too short for so big a mare.'

'She'll do,' answered Joshua; 'there's no great weight behind.'

'I've put in a keg of "Magpie" ale,' said the landlord. 'There's a confirmation at St. Kerian to-morrow, and perhaps the bishop might like it. He was very partial to it, I mind, when he was here once before—that is, before ever he was a bishop.'

'I didn't reckon on that extra weight,' said Joshua; 'I'll tighten the breeching another hole.'

'You can't do it,' answered his father, 'the buckle is at its furthest.'

'Then take out the keg of ale.'

'It would nigh kill the bishop with disappointment. I know for sure he's got this here confirmation at St. Kerian just to be near where he can taste "Magpie" ale. Whoever heard of one at that place before? I knew by the look of his face, when he was here, that he never enjoyed himself so heartily as tasting "Magpie" ale; and when he'd done, he was off like a long dog [greyhound] home to his missus, t'other side of England, to tell her what stuff we brewed down here.—And now, blowed if he ain't brought his missus to St. Kerian! What for? I ask. Does a bishop want his missus to help him to confirm? I know better; he's brought her into the neighbourhood to taste the "Magpie" ale. And, by George! they shall not be disappointed.'

The old innkeeper helped Josephine into the cart—a tax-cart, that was convertible in many ways, by ingenious arrangement of the seats—and then heaved up Bessie into Josephine's arms. Bessie would sit between the driver and her nurse; or, if she were cramped in that way, on Josephine's lap. Bessie was uneasy at the prancing of the mare, and looked timidly in Josephine's face for reassurance. The latter smiled and appeared to be without alarm, and indeed she had been accustomed to ride and drive since she was a young girl, and was not afraid of a skittish horse.

'Now, then, you kangaroo!' shouted Joshua, standing up, leaning forward, and lashing into Jenny, who bounded away at the touch of the whip, docile, conscious, by the feel of the reins, that they were in the hands of one who under-

stood her and would put up with no nonsense.

'It's a wonderful thing to consider,' said
Joshua, 'that there are men who can't see the
points in a horse. You show them a good beast
and a bad one, and they can't choose between
them. It is like having no ear for music; and
not knowing whether a chord is in tune or not.
Now then, Jenny, none of your tricks! Father
is rarely taken up with bullocks and heifers; so
is Cable; and I don't deny there's money to be
made out of them; but so is there money to be
made out of horses. Why should we not go in
for horses here? To me, there's something
mean in always growing bullocks and heifers;
there's no science, no art, no interest about it.
But a horse is another thing altogether. You
can throw your soul into that.—Do you know
this way to St. Kerian, miss?'

'No,' answered Josephine. 'When I came
to the "Magpie," I came along the road.'

'That's a distance of twelve miles, or twelve
and a half—two sides of a triangle.—I hope
you're well provided against wet weather, miss?
There's a storm coming on, and we shall be out
of all shelter on the moor.'

'We have wraps,' answered Josephine.

The wheels of the trap went noiselessly over
turf, and occasionally bounced over a tuft of

gorse. There were wheel-tracks here and there, and in some places boggy holes full of black water. The tracks radiated away in different directions—it was hard to say in which they most predominated and indicated the existence of a way.

'One might easily be pixy-led on the moors,' said Joshua, 'and wander for days without finding a house. I've been pixy-led myself round a field. Father had in a fresh brew of " Magpie " ale, and I drank a good deal of it, and then went off to look after a gray I had at grass. The evening was dark; and after I had got into the meadow, I wandered round and about, and about and round, for an hour, and could not find the gate. At last, when I was thoroughly stupid and mad with vexation, I stripped off my coat and turned it inside out, put it on again—and there was the gate before me!—If ever you get pixy-led, mind and turn your jacket. I've heard it spoken of by the old people, often, but never heeded it till that evening, and then I proved it.—Drat it! there comes the storm.'

A roaring, blinding rush of icy wind, laden with hail, and rain as cold as hail, came past. It was so fierce, so loud, so stinging, that Dancing Jenny was frightened or angry, and leaped and backed from it, and then stood stock still.

'Get along, you crocodile!' shouted Joshua, lashing at the mare.

But a stubborn fit had come on Jenny. They were on an exposed moor, without rock or tree or hedge to break the force of the gale. The hail swept by them in sheets—it spun along the ground; it cut them as if the ice-particles were small-shot. To face the wind would have been impossible. It shook the cart, and threatened to throw it over.

'By Jove!' said Joshua, 'after all, father was right to ballast us with the "Magpie" ale. There's a dip yonder in the moor; we'll down into that, and get under the lee of the hill.—Go on, you blackguardess!' And raising his whip over his head, he lashed Jenny with all the force of his arm. The mare, alarmed at the roar and force of the storm, stung with the hail on her skin, then tender, as she had been clipped and singed the day before, reared at the blow, and with a snort of anger, dashed away with the trap down the slope. Joshua put the whip between his teeth, and held the reins with both hands; the decline became sharp, the wheels danced over the tufts of gorse, tore through brakes of heather, sprang into the air over a node of quartz rock. 'Just like an Australian buck-jumper,' laughed Joshua—then Jenny was floundering in a bog, and snap—something must have given way. What then ensued, neither Josephine nor Joshua nor Bessie remembered.

They had a recollection of a hammering at the splashboard, of a crash; and when Josephine collected her scattered senses, she, clinging to Bessie, and Bessie clinging to her, lay in the marsh, and Joshua some way off, motionless; and Dancing Jenny had kicked the gig to pieces, and was tearing away with the broken shafts dangling at her sides. But Josephine only caught one glimpse of her in a lull of the storm, and then down the moor-gully rushed the hail and rain again, like water pouring out of a sluice in a canal-lock. About her were thousands of white cotton-grass heads lying prostrate before the wind, shivering, bobbing, as though the whole surface were covered with froth from the sea in flakes, or clots of snow. The cart was kicked to merest fragments—a wheel here, another with the axle there, the splashboard torn to shreds, the seat flung into the midst of the swamp, back-rail downwards, and the bottom and sides of the cart as though hacked to pieces with an axe for firewood. The breeching had given way, and the cart had touched the hocks of Jenny, driving the mare, already frightened, into a paroxysm of mad terror.

Josephine's first thought was for Bessie. The child was unhurt though shaken; and when Josephine rose to her feet, she found that she also had been jarred by the fall, though no

bones were broken or cuts inflicted. Her limbs
trembled as with bitter cold, and a sickly faint-
ness came over her, that prevented her from
gathering together her wits and deciding what
was to be done in the emergency. The effort
to stand against the wind and hail was more
than she could make, and she sank to her knees.
'Lie still,' she said to Bessie, and drew her
shawl over the child, to shelter her from the
icy blast and needle-pricking hail. Even kneeling, with her side to the wind, she had hard ado
to keep herself from being blown over, and she
held to some rushes for support that were tufted
with a coarse flower. The gale spent itself, at
all events momentarily, and the driving hail
seemed to be lifted, as a muslin veil, and beneath
it Josephine could see Joshua lying motionless,
as she had seen him in the first moment of
returning consciousness.

'Will you remain here, Bessie, whilst I go
to poor Mr. Joshua? He is hurt badly.' The
child gave a sign of consent; and Josephine,
half standing, half kneeling, staggered along to
the prostrate man. He was unconscious; he
had fallen on hard ground, not in the marsh.
No blood flowed; therefore, he had not been
cut; but she was unable to guess the extent of
his injuries. The hail was over his face, thawing
with the rain into long trickles; his waistcoat,

arms, and legs, were capped with an incrustation
of ice.

What was to be done? She could not leave
him. She could not leave Bessie to run for aid.
She did not know whence aid was obtainable.
The utmost she could do was to get the cushions
of the gig and lay one under his head. Then
she went back to Bessie.

'My darling,' she said, ' can you walk ? '

'Yes ; but not far.'

'We must do our best. The worst of the
hailstorm is over. Come with me; we must
find some men who can remove Mr. Joshua.'

'But where are they to be found ? '

Josephine considered for a moment, standing
with her back to the wind, with her hand to
her head. She could not go down the valley,
because it seemed to be nothing but a wide
spreading swamp. To return over the way she
had come would be to face the tearing wind,
and would be ineffectual, because in coming so
far they had not passed a house. The only
chance of meeting with human beings was in
going forward. Bessie must come with her.
She could not leave the child to shiver in the
cold beside the prostrate man, who might, for
all she knew, be a corpse. So she took Bessie's
hand, and encouraged her to step out bravely.
The child was frightened, cold, shaken by the

fall; but she had a stout heart, and promised to walk and keep up as much as she was able.

She returned up the slope, following the wheel-tracks the trap had made in the spongy soil, to where it had diverged from a direct course. Then she followed what she believed to be the traces of former traffic, in the presumed direction of St. Kerian. She looked about her. On all sides where she could see, where the passage of the storm had not made a blot over sky and horizon, was undulating moor, with here and there a hump of granite standing up through the moss and turf. Not a sign of the horse; not a trace of human industry. The curlews were screaming, and a flight of gulls overhead winged their way inland. Here and there, some sheep stood, clustered on the lee side of a granite block.

'Halloo, there!'

Before Josephine had seen a man, she was startled by his salutation. Now she saw him, cowering against a piece of rock, gray-habited, of the colour of the stone.

She went to him at once. 'There has been an accident. Only a few yards away, down that hollow, a man has been thrown from his gig and hurt. He is insensible. Mr. Joshua Corye —I dare say you know him.'

'What!—of the "Magpie"?'

'Yes, of the 'Magpie,''

'I know him.   Is he killed?'

'I do not know.   Do go at once to him.'

'I must get help.   Where is it?'

She indicated the exact spot.   'I will go with you and show you.'

'No,' said the shepherd; 'you go on with the child to my cot.   You can't miss it.   Keep right forward; and when you come to the Long Man——'

'The Long Man?'

'Ay, the Long Man—turn sharp to the right, and a hundred paces off you'll find some peat-works; skirt them, and you'll come on my cabin.   There's a turf-fire in it.   Warm yourself and the child, till we've got Mr. Joshua right. I must go after help, and may be some time away.'

'But—the Long Man?'

'Of course—you know the Long Man of Carnvean.   Every fool knows that.   Turn to the right at the Long Man—you can't fail.   A blind jackass would find the way.'   Then the shepherd strode away in quest of help.

That *Man* was the Cornish for stone; and that the Long Man was a stone pillar, a rude primeval granite obelisk, never for a moment occurred to Josephine.   She supposed that the shepherd pointed out the way to a fellow-shep-

herd who would give her the requisite directions,
if she forgot those already communicated. So
she went on, holding Bessie's hand, in the course
pointed out by the shepherd. Whether she
came to the monolith or not, she did not remember afterwards; she was not looking out
for one, but for a tall shepherd, and she was
not at that moment possessed with keen enthu-
siasm for prehistoric antiquities. She went on,
feeling Bessie dragging more and more at her
hand, till the little girl burst into a flood of
tears.

'What is the matter, Bessie dear?'

'I cannot go another step—my back hurts
me.'

Josephine stood still. What was to be done
now? 'The distance cannot be great. We
shall find the Long Man soon, and he will carry
you. Stay! Will you let me take you in my
arms? There; throw your arms round my
neck, and cling tightly; lay your head on my
shoulder, and I will carry you. It is not for
far. We are sure to come to the tall shepherd
in a minute.'

But no man was visible, tall or short. Josephine's knees gave way under the weight. She
was not strong, and was herself tired and bruised
and shaken, and was ill-suited to carry an addi-
tional burden to her own weary body. Then,

suddenly, they were wrapt in dense mist; it came rolling down on them like a solid wall of white wool; and in a moment they were enveloped, and could not see two paces before them. With the descent of the vapour, every idea of direction was swept away. No distance could be seen on any side; no sky, only a little circle of earth, and that through a drift of whirling watery particles. The sense first produced was one of suffocation, then of chill penetrating to the marrow.

'Bessie,' said Josephine, 'I do not know where to go whilst this fog lasts. I will lay the rug on the ground and wrap you round in it, and wait.'

The child was too frightened and weary to object. Josephine wrapped her round and laid her on the wet moss, and then threw herself down beside her. It was impossible for her to find her way. She would only over-exert herself and fall fainting with her load, if she tried to go on. There was nothing for her to do but wait. The ground was frosted with hailstones that showed no token of melting. The earth was black as soot, peaty, full of water, that oozed up under their weight—black water, smelling of bog. A stunted growth of whortleberry grew over it, and rushes; every blade of vegetation dripped with water, where not weighed down with hailstones cemented together. The mist penetrated everywhere; nothing could keep it out. Josephine was wet to the skin; her hands were numbed and aching with cold; her teeth chattered. She rose.

'My dear Bessie,' she said, 'we must make another attempt. There is no token of the fog dispersing. If I could only make out the direction of the wind, it would be some guide. Nothing can be worse than this. Let us make a push on. Now I will try to carry you on my back. I can manage that better than in my arms, at least it will be a change.'

So they struggled on. Josephine was warmed by the exertion; but she soon felt that her strength was not equal to more; and she halted with shaking knees, and looked about her.

Then Bessie uttered a cry of terror. What was it? Through the vapour loomed a gigantic figure, huge as an elephant. It moved—and in another moment Bessie and her bearer saw a sheep run past them. The fog had marvellous powers of magnifying objects seen through its veil.

'There—there is the cabin!' exclaimed Josephine, and hurried forward—to disappointment. She found a huge pile of granite rocks, weathered into layers like strata of aqueous deposits, moss-covered, split into fragments

vertically, and with fallen masses, like tables
thrown over and leaning on one another. At
all events some shelter was to be had among
these rocks, and Josephine scrambled into a cleft,
and took Bessie on her lap and laid her head on
her bosom. Her bosom was wet, but it was
warm. The little girl moaned but did not speak.
Josephine looked at her face. The eyes were
closed. 'Bessie dear?' Then the eyes opened,
and shut wearily again.

Josephine sat in the rocky cleft and looked
out. The mist drove by like smoke, smoke
thick as though the moor were on fire, and the
mist had a peaty smell. Where she was, Josephine did not know in the least. Lest she should
have gone along westward and strayed far from
St. Kerian, farther than when she started, was
her fear.

The day was closing in, and closing rapidly. She had a watch, and looked at it,
but found that it had stopped when she was
thrown from the gig. She was too tired to
speak to Bessie. She could not give her hopes, for
she could not frame them herself. If the shepherd came to his hut and found that she wasn't
there, he would look for her; but where was
he to look? How to find her in such a vapour?
She had been hot with carrying Bessie; now,
again, she was cold, bitterly cold, and cramp

came in her feet and arms. She tried to move; but Bessie uttered a fretful cry, and Josephine, on looking at her, found that she had fallen asleep. She sat on, leaning back on the rock, looking out with stagnant mind at the driving fog, shuddering convulsively at intervals with cold and exhaustion, listening to the sob and wail of the wet wind that played about the rocks and blew through its crevices. The ground fell away below the rocks rapidly, but whither she did not know, and conjectured into a ' clatter ' —that is, a ruin of granite masses difficult to thread in open day, impossible in fog and dusk. With every wave of vapour a fresh fold of darkness came on. Night was setting in rapidly.

Many hours had elapsed since either Josephine or the child had eaten anything. Bessie fortunately slept. Josephine was not hungry, but faint. She ached in every limb. So great was her exhaustion, that she had difficulty in keeping her senses from sliding away into unconsciousness. The cold weighed on her like a crown of ice, and she had to summon all her resolution not to fall asleep or faint—she knew not which would ensue.

What would happen if they spent the night on the moor? Would they be alive by morning? For herself, she did not care. All her concern was for Bessie, who was intrusted to her, and for whom she felt herself responsible. She had sinned against Richard Cable so heavily, that if she failed to keep safe and restore sound to him his dear little child, the chance of his forgiving her would be gone for ever. Then she remembered how that often when at St. Kerian she had seen the moor covered with cloud when the air was clear in the valley. The only prospect of life lay in escape from the vapour, and the only possibility of doing that was to descend from the moor.

She was so spent with cold and hunger and weariness, that she was obliged to do battle with herself before she could muster resolution to rise and recommence her wanderings. Her joints were so stiff that she cried with pain as she got out of her sitting posture, in which she had, as it were, hardened; she hardly knew if Bessie were awake or asleep, she was so silent. Round her neck, Josephine had tied Richard's blue handkerchief, as a protection from the cold, and it hung down in a point behind. She had laid Bessie on the ground before her, between her and the entrance to the rift. She knelt up, and unknotted the kerchief.

'I have been pixy-led,' she said, and sobbed with cold as she spoke; 'I will turn the kerchief.' She held it out above her head, unfolded it, gave it a toss, and reversed it, and replaced it about her shoulders. At that moment the cloud-veil parted before the rocks, and through the falling night she looked down as into a lower world, and in the blackness of a valley that seemed without bottom, saw a twinkle of many points of light. 'One—two—three—four—five —six—seven!' She uttered a gasp of relief, she could not cry. 'Bessie! dearest! Red Windows.'

## CHAPTER LIX.

### AGAIN : JACOB'S LADDER.

To Richard Cable, broken and softened, the arrival of Bishop Sellwood was welcome. The bishop was staying at the parsonage, and had walked up to Red Windows to see Cable. When Richard arrived at his gate, he saw the bishop in the garden talking to the girls and Mrs. Cable, his kind face beaming with pleasure. He came forward at once to meet Richard, and seeing that something had affected Richard, asked to have a talk with him in the garden-house, instead of going indoors. Then Richard told him frankly all his story, laying most stress on his trouble about Mary, and his fear that he had broken her heart and turned away her affection from him.

'For the matter of that,' said the bishop, 'do not be downcast. The girl is little over seventeen, and though she feels acutely at that age, the feeling is transitory; and before the year is out she will have recovered. It will all turn out for the best.  Troubles come on us all, and deepen, where without them there might be shallowness.—And now—about Josephine?'

Then Richard Cable was silent for a few minutes, looking out of the door of his summer-house; but presently he drew a long sigh and said: 'My lord, will you and Mrs. Sellwood be with us to-morrow evening?'

'I will answer for her and myself.'  Then, seeing that Cable did not desire further to pursue the subject, the bishop said: 'By the way, Mr. Cornellis has played us a nasty trick.  He got introduced somehow to Mrs. Sellwood's sister, Miss Otterbourne, quite an old lady, and married her.  She was pretty nearly twenty years his senior, and did not survive her marriage long.  My boy was to have been her heir; but she had the disposal of her property, and she has bequeathed it all to Cornellis, so my son is left out in the cold.  It is of course a bitter disappointment to us, to my wife especially; but—it is all for the best.  I hate reckoning on dead folk's shoes; it always leads to disappointment; and in this case I really believe it likely to do good, for Captain Sellwood has been somewhat inert, as he had this Bewdley estate to fall back on.  Now, he is thrown on his own resources, and roused to action.  Cable—do you remember once how he went over the palings like a greyhound? When roused, he is energetic, but only when roused. This failure of his hopes has woke him up, and he has returned to India, and I believe will distinguish himself there, for he has famous abilities, which only need calling forth.' Then he stood up. 'All right, my friend. Mrs. Sellwood and I will be with you to-morrow evening, honour bright. Wring my neck, if I forget it!'

All next day the Cable girls were busy with the house, decorating it. Their father, full of excitement, urged them on. The bishop was coming to spend the evening with them, and so 'WELCOME' must be written up in letters of green leaves and flowers in the hall. Pots of red pelargoniums and variegated geraniums must be set about to decorate the entrance. A good supper must be prepared, and plenty of lights got ready.

'Let us have all the lamps and candles that can be spared set round the entrance hall,' said Richard; 'and then, with the flowers and green leaves, it will look bright and welcoming. And —girls, mind you all put on your white confirmation dresses. You are to be confirmed to-morrow; but you must wear them also this evening.'

'Bessie is not here.'

'Bessie will be here.—Mother, mind that

her white dress be laid out for her ready, and also that other white dress of satin you spoke to me about.'

'When will Bessie be here?'

'I cannot say.—Do you hear what a storm is raging? Mr. Joshua Corye is going to drive her over, and you do not suppose that he will bring her till the worst of the weather is past. If she arrives in the afternoon, it will be well.'

The afternoon passed, and she did not arrive. Towards nightfall, a boy arrived on a moor-pony, without saddle, with a message. 'Please—Mr. Joshua was thrown out of the tax-cart, and took up insensible. He's better, and eating and drinking hearty-like now.'

'Well—and is there no further message?'

The boy looked stupid. 'Can't mind what it was,' he said. 'I lost my cap; I couldn't hold the pony in.' He was capless, with his hair flying as shaggy as the mane of the pony. The rest of the message had been blown away with his cap.

Then Richard Cable, impatient, but hardly uneasy, went to his stable and harnessed his cob into a trap he had, and just as he was about to start, the bishop came up. After a hasty explanation Dr. Sellwood said: 'Give me a hand, Cable; I will come with you; I want to tell of a plan my wife and I have formed.'

Cable helped the bishop in. 'There will be room for all,' he said, and whipped the horse.

'I want you to let Mrs. Sellwood carry Mary off,' said the bishop. 'She is a dear sweet girl; and just now is better away from St. Kerian. I hinted something of the sort to her, and a twinkle came into her face. There is nothing like change of scene and association for curing a heartache. Bless me! Cable, troubles are like stiles—made to be got over. She shall spend a month or six weeks with us; and you will see, when we send her home to you, she will have freshened up like roses after rain.' The same good considerate man as bishop as he had been as rector.

'You are very kind,' said Cable, readily touched in his present mood—'every one, indeed, is kind; I alone seem the one who has been hard and harsh.'

Richard Cable drove by the road, because he could spin along it at a fast trot; whereas over the moor, with night closing in and with a fog gathering, he would not venture. By the time he reached the 'Magpie,' night had set in; but the effects of the storm were dispersing, the mists were clearing, and the sky shining, with its many stars.

'Well,' said Cable, drawing up at the 'Magpie' door, 'where are they?'

'What?' asked Corye, coming out. 'Are they not with you?'

Then only did Cable learn the whole story of the accident. Joshua was better; he was put to bed, but vowed he would be up and take a ride next day.

'He's got such a constitution!' explained his father. 'He's been brought up on "Magpie" ale.'

'But—where are Bessie and the other one?'

'That is more than I can tell. They sent Zackie Martin the shepherd after my Joshua. and walked on themselves towards St. Kerian.'

'But they have not arrived.'

'Lord bless you! they are there by this time. Did you not pass them? Which way did you come?'

'By the road.'

'Well, that accounts for your missing them. They went the short way over the moor.'

'But Bessie could not walk so far. Where did the accident take place?'

'This side of the Long Man. Zackie told them the way and how to reach his hut, where there was a fire; but, I reckon, they tired of waiting and went on.'

'They have not arrived. Bessie could not walk so far.'

'Go home over the moor; you'll find them at Red Windows, sure as boys go to stables.—It's a mercy my Joshua wasn't more hurt. He was quite stupid for an hour.'

Nothing more was to be got out of the inn-keeper. Cable became seriously alarmed. He asked for a light for his lamps, and started over Carnvean Down. He knew the way; he had ridden it and driven it scores of times. He was silent now, and the bishop respected his anxiety. Trails of fog still drifted over the high moorland, but they were speedily passed through; they were lifting in the cold night-air. Occasionally, Cable shouted, but received no answer.

'There is the Long Man,' he said, pointing with his whip to the stone, that rose about sixteen feet above the turf. 'If they are wandering anywhere about, they will see the lamps; we must not go too fast.' Nevertheless, ever and anon Richard urged on the horse. He was nervous; he did not know what to think, whether they were lost on the down, or had pressed on. 'You see,' he said, 'Bessie could not go fast. *She*—that other—must tarry for her; so we may find them at home. I should have wished to have been there to meet them.'

They were an hour crossing the moor. As they came to the descent—'Look!' said Richard. 'Before I started, I told them to light a candle in every window upstairs. One, two, three, four, five, six—seven lights.'

'Yes, I see; quite an illumination,' said Dr. Sellwood.

'And I told them to have a blaze of lamps and candles in the hall, that when they came in and out of the dark, it would be to welcome light and warmth. Please God they are safe!'

'Amen!' responded the bishop.

When they came to the gate, which •was open, Cable fastened his horse to it. 'I will not take him out till I know they have arrived,' he said, and walked on over the gravel path to the foot of the flight of stone steps that led to the front door. Then, all at once, he, going before the bishop, uttered a cry, and stood still.

'What is the matter?' asked Dr. Sellwood, pressing forward.

They saw in the dark a black heap at the foot of the steps.

'It is they—it is they! They are dead!' cried Richard, quite unmanned and beside himself.

Then the bishop ran back to the tax-cart, and removed one of the lanterns, and came with it hastily to where the heap lay. Cable was as one frozen to the ground, unable to act through overwhelming terror and sorrow. The bishop knelt, and drew back a thick shawl; then the

light of the lamp fell on the face of a child, and
the child moved, uttered a moan, opened its
eyes, and turned them away again.

'It is Bessie!' groaned Cable.

'She is alive,' said the bishop.   He gently
disengaged her from the arms of Josephine, and
for a moment laid her on the ground, then he
felt the pulse and looked at Josephine.   Then
he took up Bessie again, and said in a low,
shaking voice : 'Cable—I will carry the child
in.   She is in no immediate danger.   It is other
with Josephine—your wife.   I must get your
mother to bring her a cordial at once.   There
is hardly any pulse, scarcely breath left.   She
is sinking from over-exhaustion ; and I do not
know whether she will live or not.   You stay
by her ; you alone can save her.   The soul is
fluttering on her lips to depart ; try to stay it.
—I will send for a doctor ; but her fate will be
settled one way or the other before he comes.'
He had set the carriage lantern against the first
step ; the end, unperceived by him, was on the
shawl, and as he lifted Bessie, he drew the shawl
away and upset the lantern, which was extinguished.   Holding the little crippled girl in his
arms, he ascended the flight of steps and struck
at the front door, that flew open ; and he was
dazzled with the blaze of many lights, and the
sight of the young girls standing there all in

white. 'My dears,' he said, 'I have Bessie;
she is safe. Your father is below; he wants
light.—Quick!    Go to him, and—and kiss
your *mother*.'    Then he pushed past them with
his burden, calling for Mrs. Cable.

Below, in the darkness, at the foot of the
flight of stone steps that led up to the house,
was Richard Cable, half kneeling, half-sitting,
staying up Josephine in his arms, holding her to
his heart, trembling, sobbing, crying out of the
depths of his heart to God to help him.    Then,
in choking voice, with a struggle to force the
tones, as he held the hardly conscious form
in his arms, he began to sing the melody—not
the words, which he did not know, but the air
of the Mermaid's song, swaying her to the ca-
dence of the tune, as if she were a babe he was
hushing to sleep.    Was he lulling her to her
eternal sleep?    Was she dying in his arms?
O! Infinitely precious, unspeakably dear was
she to him now, that he seemed about to lose
her.    All the suppressed love for her, the love
driven back by his iron will, returned and rolled
through heart and veins as the bore in the
Severn.    Still he sang on, with broken voice, the
Mermaid's air.    And as he thus sang and swayed
her, down the stairs from the brilliantly illumined
hall came the six girls, all in white, and each
carried a light—Mary first, then Effie, then Jane,

Martha next, and Lettice, lastly Susie. In their haste to obey the bishop and to assist their father, each had caught up a light; and so, each carrying a light in the still air, under the stars of night, the six girls in white came down the steps to where their father held the exhausted Josephine. They came round her, each holding her light. Josephine opened her eyes feebly, scarce conscious that she saw aught; then Mary stepped timidly up to her and kissed her, and passed on; then Effie and she went by; and Jane kissed her, stooping, and holding her light; and Martha next; and after her Lettice; and last of all, little Susie.

Did Josephine recall an evening in the cottage at Hanford, when Cable had bidden his children—the same six—walk round her in the sunlight, and not approach, not touch her? No; her mind was too dead with exhaustion to remember aught.

But Josephine's eyes opened wide; the soft warm kisses of the children and the light roused her failing spirit, and the open eyes looked, no longer with the glaze of death on them, but with a far-away, searching, earnest longing—*upwards*, into the dark sky, set with ten thousand points of light.

'Josephine!' said Richard Cable—'Josephine!' It was the first—the only time he had uttered her name since they parted on the night that he sought her at Brentwood Hall.

She did not answer. She had not strength to answer; but a slight movement was visible on her lips; and as the children stood with the circle of light round her, and Cable looked down into her white upturned face, he saw water rise in the eyes that had been dry, and brim them, and run over the long lower lashes, but they never fell, for he stooped and received them on his lips.

Then the bishop appeared with something Mrs. Cable had given him for Josephine to take, whilst she attended to little Bessie. 'She may be carried in now,' said Dr. Sellwood. 'Richard has brought her back from the brink of the grave.'

# CHAPTER LX.

## TWICE MARRIED.

'And now, sir—I mean, my lord—I shall venture to ask you to marry me again,' said Richard Cable to the bishop, the evening after the confirmation.

'Good gracious, Cable!' Dr. Sellwood started.

'Well,' said Cable, in his leisurely, resolute way, 'now that Josephine is recovering, I should like to be married again.'

'Married again!' Dr. Sellwood's rosy face became mottled.

'Well, my lord,' said Cable, 'you see—before, it was Josephine married me; and now, *I* want to marry *her.*'

'But you are married. It can't be done.'

'Why not? It is not bigamy, is it, to be married twice to the same woman?'

'Bigamy—good gracious!—it looks something like it; and etymologically——'

'I beg your pardon, sir—I mean, my lord —I do not understand.'

'According to the derivation of the word from the original Greek, it does make it a case of bigamy.'

'But I cannot be punished for it—can I?'

'No; hardly that.'

'Or you for marrying me again?'

'No; hardly.'

'Then bigamy or no bigamy, I wish to be remarried.—You see, it will be good several ways. Folks at St. Kerian never knew that Josephine was my wife; and they would ask questions and talk, and want to worry out all our past troubles and differences, if I were simply to declare we had been married, but separated. Whereas, if we get married here, in the church, publicly, no one will think to ask any questions, and there will be no nose-poking into the past, to cause Josephine and me annoyance.'

'There is something in this.—I will turn it over in my head. Of course the registers could not be used, but the ceremony.—I will write and ask my lawyer.—How is little Bessie?'

'Failing,' said Cable. 'I am about, I suppose, now to build up anew my domestic life, and I have laid the foundation in my first-born, and shall set up the gates in my youngest.'

'As for Mary,' said the bishop confidently

—' no such thing. She'll get over this matter much more speedily than you imagine, and not a bit of her love to you will be lost. Take my word for it, all will come right in the end. You are going to lend her to us for six weeks.'

'Why!' exclaimed Richard ; 'Good gracious me ! it must be for another reason.'

'What must be ? '

'My bigamy.'

'Why ?   What is the second reason ? '

'All is prepared for it—to the bridesmaids' dresses.  My daughters have their confirmation garments, and Josephine her white satin wedding gown, laid out upstairs all ready.'

.     .     .     .     .

Two years have passed.  Richard Cable is the Richard Cable of old in gentleness, tenderness ; all the sullenness and bitterness have passed away completely.  But he is not the Richard Cable of old altogether, for there is a refinement of manner about him which he lacked when our story began and we first encountered him. But Josephine is very much altered from the Josephine with whom we made acquaintance on the lightship, now full of love and forbearance, and that ineffable sweetness and charm which only self-conquest and suffering can give.

'Richard,' said she one morning at breakfast, 'what is to be done?—Now that my poor father is dead, and the death was very sudden, Bewdley comes to me. I am continually coming in for estates to which I have no right.'

'Do you remember how the bishop told us we were to cease knocking our heads together about Hanford! Now we have that, we do not want more.'

'No; I have no right to Bewdley. I shall make it over to Captain Sellwood, just as I made over Hanford to you.'

'Perhaps he will act as I did.'

Josephine sat dreamily opening the letter just arrived by post. All at once her interest was aroused, her colour mounted, and her eye sparkled.

'What is it, Josephine?'

'This difficulty settles itself.'

'How so?'

'Look, Richard! Here is a letter from Mrs. Sellwood.'

'How is Mary? When is she coming back? She spends half her time with the Sellwoods.'

'Look, Richard!—Mrs. Sellwood—— But do read, dear Richard.' She sat looking eagerly in his face as he deciphered the not very intelligible writing of the bishop's wife. Then his colour came, and his eyes sparkled.

'Well,' said Josephine, 'does it not settle itself?'

'Not at all. Bewdley is yours, and Mary is my daughter.'

'Nonsense, Richard. There is no mine and thine between us, but all things are in common. —What do you say?'

'The bishop was right. Mary is consoled for the loss of Walter Penrose.'

'He is right. He always said: All will turn out well in the end.'

'And what can be better than that Captain Sellwood, who has come back from India, should have *our* dear Mary, and with her, that *we* should give him Bewdley?'

THE END.

PRINTED BY
SPOTTISWOODE AND CO., NEW-STREET SQUARE
LONDON